About the Author

George Owen, author of 'The Shadow of an Artist', was born in Boston, Massachusetts. He grew up in Massachusetts and New Hampshire and went to the University of New Hampshire. He now resides in Ponte Vedra Beach, Florida. During his varied career, he was a newspaper reporter for the Manchester Union Leader, the Lowell Sun, and the Florida Times-Union. An avid photographer, he has traveled to a number of countries in South America, Europe, and China, and has published a book of photographs, "Faces of Latin America." He often goes back to Paris, and since 1972, he has returned more than a dozen times.

The Shadow of an Artist

George Owen

The Shadow of an Artist

Olympia Publishers
London

www.olympiapublishers.com
OLYMPIA PAPERBACK EDITION

A CIP catalogue record for this title is
available from the British Library.

ISBN: 978-1-80439-837-1

This is a work of fiction.
Names, characters, places, and incidents originate from the writer's imagination. Any resemblance to actual persons, living or dead, is purely
coincidental.

First Published in 2024

Olympia Publishers
Tallis House
2 Tallis Street
London
EC4Y 0AB

Printed in Great Britain

Acknowledgements

In writing The Shadow of an Artist', I relied on a number of historical sources. They include: Beth Archer Brombert's "Édouard Manet Rebel in a Frock Coat", Sue Roe's "The Private Lives of the Impressionists", Jeffrey Meyers' "Impressionist Quartet"; John Rewald's "The History of Impressionism"; Nigel Gosling's "Nadar"; "Berthe Morisot Correspondence" edited by Denis Rouart; "Manet By Himself" edited by Juliet Wilson-Bareau; Henry Sutherland Edward s' "Old and New Paris": Patricia Wright's "Manet;" Antonin Proust's "Édouard Manet: Souvenirs;" George Bataille's "Manet"; Theodore Duet's "History of Édouard Manet and His Work"; Percival J. Brine's "The Revolution and Siege of Paris"; the web site "Manet.org"; Ross King's "The Judgement of Paris"; T.J. Clark's "The Painting of Modern Life"; The Metropolitan Museum of Art's "Manet 1832-1883"; and Charles Baudelaire's poem "The Rope".

"Everything is mere appearance, the pleasures of a passing hour, a midsummer night's dream. Only painting, the reflection of a reflection - but the reflection, too, of eternity – can record some of the glitter of this mirage."
~ Édouard Manet

Prologue

My great-grandfather, Jules Marchand, was a close friend of the painter Édouard Manet who died at fifty-one of complications from syphilis. The pallbearers at Édouard 's funeral were some of the great artists of their time; the novelist Emile Zola, the painter Claude Monet, the photographer Felix Nadar, and my great-grandfather.

A year after Édouard Manet's death, my great-grandfather began a novel based on their thirty-five-year friendship. For almost nine years, he worked on the novel, picking it up and putting it down many times. But he did not finish it. Almost ten years after the death of Édouard Manet, my great-grandfather, at sixty-two, suffered a heart attack and died.

The unfinished manuscript, along with Édouard Manet's journal and several of my great-grandfather's writings were found in a trunk hidden away in a Paris attic. For more than two years, I traveled back and forth between Paris and New York, where I was living, determined to claim the trunk and its contents; after much litigation, the court granted me ownership.

As an art student in Paris, I had always been interested in Édouard Manet. When I learned of the trunk being found, I became obsessed with translating, finishing, and publishing the manuscript as a novel. It was a great challenge, especially because I wanted to include some of Manet's journal entries. I hope I have done both the manuscript and the journal entries justice.

The day I opened the trunk and thumbed through the manuscript I found a note in my great-grandfather's handwriting. It read: "Even though this is a work of fiction, much of it is based on fact. I hope when I finish it and it is published anyone who reads it will appreciate the life of the greatest painter of the nineteenth century and recognize his contribution to the world of art."

Chapter One

Memories of a thirty-five-year friendship streamed through his mind as Julian Mercier stood with hundreds of other mourners at the funeral of Édouard Manet. He watched the light spilling through the church's stained-glass windows fluttering images of faith, hope, and charity, absent the glow of Édouard's paintings.

The Archbishop of Paris, along with the parish priest, a deacon, and several acolytes, proceeded with a Solemn High Mass. It was not appropriate for someone who was baptized but, on his deathbed, refused last rites; Édouard Manet was a man not easily understood.

Julian took out a letter from his coat pocket that Édouard had given him a few days before his death. But then he put it back into his pocket. He would read it after Édouard was buried.

Thirteen years before, February 20, 1870, one of the coldest days in memory, Julian and Édouard hurried into the Café Guerbois. Julian's toes felt frostbitten and Édouard had a hacking cough. After they had taken off their hats, scarves, and coats, a waiter ushered them to their usual table. More than a hundred people occupied cheap metal chairs, sitting around marble-topped tables that crammed the noisy, smoke-filled café.

The waiter took Édouard and Julian's orders and returned in minutes, balancing a tray over his head with two bowls of soup resting on it. Slowly, the waiter lowered the tray, putting it down on a nearby stand. He picked up the two bowls, one in each hand, and then set one down in front of Julian and the other in front of

Édouard.

"Is there anything else?" the waiter asked.

Édouard, who was reading his newspaper, looked up and then at the table. "Young man, I don't see any bread."

"I'm sorry, sir."

The waiter grabbed the tray, quickly turned around, and headed back to the kitchen. In less than five minutes, he returned with a basket filled with bread and a plateful of butter, setting them down on the table in front of Édouard.

"That's a good man," Édouard said before he began to cough again.

"Are you all right?" Julian asked.

"It's this frigid weather. It's given me a cold and I can't get rid of it."

"What did you say?" Julian asked, not hearing Édouard clearly because of the noise from all the people talking around them.

"Yes. I'm fine. Is it any good?" Édouard asked.

"What did you say?"

"Is the soup any good?"

"Good as usual."

"For a writer, you're a man of few words," Édouard said, with a smile on his face.

Julian was silent for a moment. How had their friendship survived the last twenty two years, from the day they met in 1848? He spoke less reducing the chance of stuttering, but not a man of few words, who earned a good living writing for a half dozen Paris journals.

Julian looked straight into Édouard's eyes. "You know why I don't talk much. It's my stuttering. I think it's getting worse. It's just like your whistling."

"No, your stuttering is not getting worse. What did you say about my whistling?"

"You whistle when you're nervous. "It's the same song every time. You whistle the Traviata drinking song and you're off-key when you do."

"I don't whistle that much."

"All right, you don't do it that much, and I rarely stammer. But you know it bothers me when people stare and sometimes laugh at me. I try to hide my stammering because people like to find fault in others while forgetting their own flaws."

"You're right. I've told you I feel the same way when someone laughs at me or criticizes one of my paintings, especially if it's a woman."

"You've never been able to tell me why, especially a woman."

"That's because I don't know why."

"There's got to be a reason."

"I haven't been able to figure it out," Édouard said. "Now, if you don't mind, I'm going to go back to reading my newspaper and you can continue slurping your soup."

A few minutes went by and Julian heard Édouard's newspaper hitting the table. He looked up and watched Édouard jump up from his chair.

"What does that puppeteer know about art?" Édouard shouted.

"What's wrong?"

"This man criticizes my paintings. But all he can do is pen worthless dramas performed by marionettes at his puppet theatre."

"What are you talking about?"

"Louis Duranty. The puppet master poet of the Tuileries who

15

is also a lousy art critic."

"What do you mean?"

Édouard grabbed his newspaper from the table and stabbed with one finger at an article he had been reading. "It's blasphemy, this sentence he wrote about my paintings."

"Maybe he's also a man of few words."

"Don't toy with me. He's supposed to be a friend. Why did he write this? Is he here?"

"No. I haven't seen him."

"He's got some nerve, and I'm going to make him pay; I will challenge him to a duel."

"Édouard, are you out of your mind?"

"He'll be here tonight for dinner, and I will be here to challenge him to a duel. You mark my words."

Just as Édouard and Julian were about to leave, Duranty came into the café and walked directly toward them.

"Are you leaving already?" Duranty asked.

Édouard stared at Duranty. "You bastard," Édouard shouted. Everyone in the room heard him and looked up. Several people got up from their tables and stood around Édouard and Duranty.

"What do you mean, calling me a bastard?" Duranty said. Julian heard the rage in his voice.

"You know what I mean. It's what you wrote. I'm challenging you to a duel," Édouard said as reached into his coat pocket, pulled out his gloves, and slapped Duranty's face.

"You're crazy. You can't slap me."

"You're the one who's crazy."

Édouard slapped Duranty again. "I'm not going to argue with you. I demand a duel."

"Good, Manet. I agree. When and where?"

"In three days, the Saint-Germain Forest at eleven o'clock in

16

the morning, with swords."

"You better show up, Manet."

Julian pulled Édouard aside. "What are you doing? You're not sixteen. You're nearly forty.

Your ambition is going to kill you. That's what makes you angry enough to challenge Duranty."

"You should be more ambitious. That's what will make you a great writer."

"I'm ambitious enough."

Édouard stared at Duranty and shook his fist. "I'll be there and my friend Emile Zola will be my second. Who'll yours be?"

"Paul Alexis. He and Monsieur Zola are friends," Duranty said with a slight laugh. Julian was silent. Friendship wasn't at stake; someone's life was. Either Édouard or Duranty could wind up dead. None of this made any sense, although he thought about the irony of it all; two years before, when Édouard was attacked by critics for his painting, "Olympia," Zola defended him with an essay published in a prominent Paris journal and now Zola would be Édouard's second in a duel. Didn't Édouard understand?

The morning of the day of the duel, Édouard and Julian climbed into a carriage to go to Saint-Lazare station. Édouard carried a French naval officer's sword given to him on his voyage to Rio to Le Havre, the same one where Édouard and Julian, both sixteen years old, met.

Édouard was whistling when he and Julian met Zola at the train station. Zola took Édouard aside.

"Are you sure you want to go through with this, Édouard?"

"I'm more than sure."

"Édouard, think about it," Julian said. "You're going to get killed. You're not thinking straight."

"Duranty has to pay," Édouard said, his voice more

emphatic.

The train ride from Saint-Lazare station to Saint-Germain station took less than forty minutes. All that time Zola kept trying to talk Édouard out of the duel. But Édouard kept insisting there was no turning back.

After they arrived at the Saint-Germain station, it was a few minutes' walk to the forest. As they approached a clearing about twenty feet into the forest, Julian could see Duranty with his second, Paul Alexis, standing next to him. Duranty was holding a sword that looked much like the one Édouard carried.

Édouard walked briskly up to Duranty with his sword raised high in the air.

"Are you ready?"

"Yes. Are you?"

"I'm more than ready," Édouard said, as the two men faced off.

Zola and Julian stood behind Édouard, and Duranty's second stood behind him.

There was a worried look on Julian's face, although he felt some relief that Édouard told him on the train earlier that he had taken up fencing when he was young.

Julian watched the first clash of the swords, as Édouard hollered at Duranty, "Are you ready to die?

"Are you?" Duranty screamed back.

Édouard took a swipe at Duranty but missed him by at least a foot.

"I'd hate to kill you," Édouard shouted, lifting his sword in the air again.

"I'd hate for you to die," Duranty yelled back.

Duranty plunged his sword toward Édouard's chest, but Édouard jumped out of the way.

"You think you're a superb swordsman, do you?" Édouard said.

"Better than you," Duranty hollered.

Julian continued to watch in amazement. Bundled up against the cold, he felt a drop of sweat slide down his back.

With no warning, Édouard struck his sword against Duranty's chest. He wounded Duranty, but it was a superficial cut. For the next several minutes, they kept going at each other. Their breathing got heavier and heavier and they both looked like they were ready to collapse. They lunged at each other, and the swords met; there was so much force behind the blows that the blades of both swords buckled.

Immediately after the clash of the swords, it was quiet, except for the sound of the wind blowing through the forest around them. Zola and Alexis walked up to the Édouard and Duranty and pushed them away from each other.

"There's no need to keep up this duel," Zola said, as he watched the two men without hesitation nod in agreement and then shake hands. Édouard looked at the wound on Duranty's chest. "Do you need a doctor?" Édouard asked.

"No. I'll be all right."

Duranty and Alexis got into a carriage waiting for them at the edge of the forest. Édouard, Zola, and Julian slowly walked back to the train station.

"I'm a pretty good swordsman. Don't you think?" Édouard said, bragging to Julian and Zola.

"You're lucky you weren't killed, or that you didn't kill Duranty," Julian said.

"You're a much better painter than you are a swordsman," Zola said.

"I'm going to convince Duranty of that," Édouard said.

A few weeks after the duel, Julian asked Édouard to join him for lunch at the Café Guerbois. Édouard couldn't go because he had to meet someone but didn't say who he was meeting. When Julian walked into the café, he was amazed to see Édouard and Duranty sitting together at a table, having lunch and laughing.

Three months later, Julian and Édouard were at the Café Guerbois having lunch. Édouard was reading a review of his paintings Duranty had written.

"What did Duranty write?" Julian asked.

"That my paintings stand out among all others and he predicted I would prove to be one of the greatest painters of the century."

"I guess you convinced him."

"Yes, I did, but there are still so many more critics I need to convince."

Chapter Two

It was twenty-two years before the duel, December 8, 1848, when Julian Mercier met Édouard Manet. That morning Julian was looking toward the sky at the great white sails of a three-masted ship. His eyes wide open, he stood waiting to board *Le Havre et Guadeloupe*. What would it be like to cross the Atlantic, to be at sea for weeks on end, to travel thousands of miles from home, land in another country, and go ashore to explore an unknown country? As he continued to gaze at the bone-white sails, he felt his neck muscles tightening. He was breathless.

On that day, Julian would begin his journey from Le Havre to Rio de Janeiro. It would also be the first day of his friendship with Édouard Manet. It would last more than three decades until Édouard's death at fifty-one. Julian stood in line with a group of boys. They were all about his age. Almost every boy had a canvas bag slung over one shoulder, packed with everything needed for the crossing. One boy ahead of Julian had a much larger bag and was better dressed than everyone else. While the other boys talked among themselves, the boy with the larger bag stood alone. Julian watched him look toward the ocean and then down at the sketch pad in his hand. He was drawing the horizon, where the ocean touched the sky.

Julian heard shouting and saw a sailor bully his way up the gangway. He shouted at the sailor, "Stop your pushing." When the sailor shoved by Julian, he looked up at his face. The sailor had a horrendous scar running from his right ear to the corner of his mouth. When the sailor reached the boy with the sketch pad, he forced his elbow into his ribs. The boy dropped to his knees and the sketch pad sailed into the water. "Don't get in my way," the sailor shouted and continued up the gangway. Slowly, the boy lifted himself up and dusted off his clothes.

"A…a-re you all right?" Julian asked.

"I got the wind knocked out of me, but I'm fine." His voice shook slightly. "A…are you sure?"

"Yes. I'm sure."

"Come on. We need to get aboard."

When they reached the deck, the sailor was nowhere in sight. It was raining, and Julian looked down at the tiny puddles of water forming around his feet before he spoke again.

"W…w-hat's your name?"

"Manet, Édouard Manet."

"Mine's Julian."

"Julian, what?"

"Mercier."

"Are you from here?"

"No. P…Paris."

"That's where I'm from."

"Y…y-you've said nothing about my stammering."

"No, and I wouldn't. It's just something I wouldn't do. Besides, you looked out for me."

"I didn't do anything."

"Yes, you did. You yelled at the sailor to stop."

"You know, I'm going to miss Paris," Julian said, ignoring the praise and finding it easier not to stammer. "Although I wish it wasn't as crowded and dirty."

"What I like about Paris is strolling the heights of Montmartre. Halfway down the slope of Rue Tourlaque, which descends abruptly, there is a cemetery I walk by, and I'm not scared. Nothing scares me."

"Nothing scares me either. But there are some things that bother me."

"Like what?"

"I hated it when some of my classmates laughed at me because I stammered," Julian said.

"I can't stand it when I'm laughed at. What did you do about it?"

"I tried to ignore them and stayed by myself. It may sound strange, but I spent a lot of my time reading."

"That's not strange. I read a lot."

"I watched you as you were sketching. You must be interested in drawing?"

"Not exactly. I'm more interested in painting. It's more important to me than anything. My ambition is to leave my mark in life as a painter."

"W…w-hat do you mean, leave your mark?"

"It's something I learned from my uncle. He took me to the Louvre many times to study the paintings. He would say in life, it's not the number of years you're on earth that matters; it's how you spend that time. You have a duty to leave your mark."

"A duty?"

"To yourself."

"So, that's important to you?"

"Just as much as painting."

Through the lashing rain, the cannons from the town thundered, while Édouard and Julian stood silent. Despite the heavy downpour, the smell of gunpowder filled the air. The cannons signaled the ship was about to leave port. Over one hundred townspeople jostled for position on the rain-soaked jetty, straining to get one last glimpse of the ship.

Édouard looked out at the crowd. "My father's out there," Édouard pointed to a short, heavy but fragile-looking man. Julian spotted the man who bore little resemblance to his slim, muscular son.

"He came to see me off, but he doesn't think much of me."

"Why do you say that?"

"He's never listened to me, and he doesn't care what I think. But maybe someday he'll respect me."

Julian was silent as he continued to watch Édouard's father shouting and jumping up and down.

"W…w-hat do you mean?" Julian asked. "My father respects me and cares what I think."

"I'll earn his respect when I join the Navy," Édouard said.

"That will make him respect you?"

"I hope so. He wanted me to study law, to follow in his footsteps. He's a judge."

"Why didn't you?"

"I wanted to be an artist. So, we compromised."

"Compromised?"

"Yes. I love the sea. I said I'd give up becoming an artist and join the Navy."

"W…w-what's wrong with being an artist?"

"He doesn't think it's an honorable profession."

The rain was beating down. Édouard looked at his father, who was now holding an umbrella. "When I come back to Paris, I'll pass the exam. You'll see," Édouard shouted.

"I'm not sure he heard you."

"Probably not."

"What are you talking about?"

"The exam for the Naval Academy. I failed it and I don't

enjoy failing. But I can take it again once I get some training on this ship, and then I'll pass it."

Julian smiled at Édouard. "That's why I'm here too. I failed the exam and felt bad about it. I promised my father after I shipped out and got the required training, I'd take the exam again. But I don't think I'd lose my father's respect if I failed it."

"You're the lucky one," Édouard said.

"Maybe."

The two watched the ship slowly pull away from the port. Soon, the town was out of sight and they were at sea. Édouard stood staring at the sea. He looked intensely at the stars and the light created by the moon on the horizon.

"What do you think of the light? Do you see the light and shadow?" Édouard asked.

"This is the first time I've seen it. I never knew it existed."

"I love to watch what the light can do."

"That's because you have the sense of an artist."

"No. I'm going to have the legs of a sailor."

The two friends laughed, and then they were quiet. The sea was getting rougher, and they watched several cadets who had gotten sick lean over the railings. Several black clouds appeared overhead, and the wind was blowing harder. Julian felt the sea pushing against the ship and could hear the wind whistling through the rigging.

"We better get inside," Julian said.

They rushed to their cabin. When Édouard opened the cabin door, they saw two sailors sitting on two of the four bunk beds in the room. They were playing cards and sharing a bottle of whiskey. One sailor took a few swigs and then passed the bottle back to the other sailor. Julian recognized one of the sailors. He was the sailor with the scar on his face who pushed Édouard to the ground.

"You fools haven't fallen overboard yet? What are you doing here?" he yelled. "This ain't your cabin."

"Y…y-es it is," Julian said.

The other sailor, who was at least fifty pounds heavier than Julian, jumped up and stared at them.

"Listen to him. I'll bet you're quite the wonder with the ladies," the heavy-set sailor said.

"Will you listen to this one?" The scar-faced sailor said. His craggy voice deepened. "The boy can't get the cork out of his mouth."

Julian stared at him, ready to fight. Suddenly, the scar-faced sailor grabbed Julian and pushed him to the floor. Édouard rushed at the sailor and hit him in the face with his clenched fist. Despite the force of the punch, the sailor stood his ground and reached into his back pocket. He pulled out a six-inch knife and waved it at Édouard.

"I'll kill you," the sailor shouted.

Édouard reached for a broom in a corner of the cabin. He picked it up and swung at the sailor.

"You bastard," the scar-faced sailor screamed as the heavy-set sailor circled Édouard and rushed him from behind.

Suddenly, the cabin door swung open, and the boatswain walked in. He saw the sailor with the knife and told him to drop it.

The sailor loosened his grip on the knife, and it fell to the floor. The boatswain picked it up and looked at it. There was a gold star embedded in the pearl handle.

"What's your name, sailor?" the boatswain asked.

"Pierre Pelleton."

"Where did you get that knife?"

"I pulled it out of a dead man."

"His back, no doubt. I'll hold on to it, and the captain will hear about this."

The boatswain moved toward Édouard and Julian. Before the boatswain said anything to them, Julian spoke up.

"S…s-ir, they said there's no room for us in the cabin."

"Don't call me sir, cadet. Calling me sir won't help."

"N…n-o, sir. I mean, yes, sir. I mean…I mean."

Édouard spoke up. "We got assigned to this cabin, and they're telling us we don't belong here."

The boatswain looked Édouard up and down. "I don't know how that happened. We don't have cadets sharing cabins with the crew. I'll get you another cabin."

Julian and Édouard grabbed their bags and walked behind the boatswain to a cabin a hundred feet down the hall. The boatswain opened the door, and a rat scurried from the room. It was half the size of the other cabin, and it smelled musty.

"This is going to be your home," the boatswain said.

"Thank you," Julian said.

"One more thing," the boatswain said. "You've made a terrible start of it, boys. You better watch yourselves,"

"We will," Édouard said.

After the boatswain left, Édouard and Julian quickly got undressed and jumped into their bunks.

Julian stayed awake for almost an hour. The scar-faced sailor who could have killed them slept just a hundred yards away and the idea that there were thousands of miles to go before reaching Rio was on his mind.

Chapter Three

The voyage seemed endless, despite the many storms that helped lessen the monotony. Julian and Édouard got sick several times, as did many of the cadets. When they weren't getting sick, the sight of sea and sky was energizing. But the long days could also be numbing and boring.

After two months, the ship entered the Rio de Janeiro harbor and glided alongside dozens of other vessels. For Édouard and Julian, it was a tremendous experience. Ships navigated through a bay entrance guarded by stone forts. The vistas were of vivid greenery capped by gray granite mountain tops. It was an hour before the ship lowered anchor. It was not until the next day that the government officials came on board. They checked everyone's papers and then allowed the cadets and the crew to go ashore.

In the bright sunlight, with the mountains above the city, Julian rowed one of the ship's dinghies he and Édouard had lowered into the water. They were excited to go ashore and walk the streets of the city. Julian had a good feeling about being on dry land, but the narrow, dirty streets and ramshackle buildings lessened the grandeur of the mountains and the sea.

"I don't see many white men," Julian said. "There are a lot of Negroes and many women with dark skin."

"They say the well-to-do Brazilian men rarely go out to walk the streets and the women even less," Édouard said. "When the women go out, they're followed by a maid or accompanied by their children."

Julian and Édouard walked by the slave market. It was a revolting sight. They sold the strongest, healthiest males individually at the highest prices. The elderly, sick, disabled, and children were sold by weight in lots.

"All the Black people are slaves," Édouard sighed. "They all look downtrodden. It's amazing what power the whites have over them."

"I think the Negro women are pretty," Julian said as he stared at a young woman who was naked to the waist, wearing a scarf tied at her neck and falling over her breasts.

"Why don't you tell her?" Édouard said.

Julian wanted to speak to her without stuttering. During the voyage, it helped to deal with his stuttering by speaking slowly and using easy words. But he thought this wasn't the right time to speak with a woman he didn't know, and who probably didn't speak his language.

Julian and Édouard continued walking through the streets of the city and the fancy neighborhoods that were part of the French enclave. Along the Rua do Ouvidor, Rio's top fashion street, they saw French-owned bookshops, cigar shops, haberdashers, hairdressers, perfumeries, and florists.

"These shops are making me homesick for Paris," Julian said.

"But they have a different taste," Édouard said.

The morning turned into the afternoon. At this time of day, all the Brazilian ladies were at their front doors or on their balconies, throwing multicolored wax balls filled with water at every man who passed by. Julian and Édouard hurled the balls back at the women.

As they continued walking, a young woman, maybe sixteen

or seventeen, who was alone, caught Édouard's attention when she smiled at him.

Julian noticed she was wearing a blouse, which was open in the front. She was tall and thin with light brown skin. Her eyes were piercing brown. She stood an inch taller than Édouard.

"I want to talk to her," Édouard said.

"You don't speak Portuguese."

"What's your name?" Édouard asked the young woman in French.

"Clarissa," she giggled.

"She must speak a little French," Edward said, nodding to Julian.

"Speak slowly," Julian said.

"Are you married?" Édouard asked.

She hesitated for a moment. Then she said, "No."

Édouard slowly put his arm around her waist and looked up to kiss her. She pressed her lips against Édouard's and smiled at him.

"I'll be back in a while," Édouard said to Julian.

Édouard held her hand, and they hurried along the cobblestone street toward a building a few hundred yards away.

"I'll meet you back at this same spot in two hours," Julian yelled to Édouard. For the next two hours, Julian spent the time visiting the bars along the street. They were not the cafes of Paris; the patrons didn't talk much, but they drank a lot. Two hours later, Julian stumbled back to the spot where he was supposed to meet Édouard, who was already there.

"Did you enjoy yourself?" Julian asked Édouard.

Julian had a grin on his face. He imagined Édouard going to bed with the girl. Édouard would slowly undress her, and she would help him get his pants off. Then he would pick her up and carry her to bed. Before Julian could imagine anything more, Édouard punched him lightly in the shoulder.

"Yes, I did," Édouard said.

"Did she like it?"

"I think she did."

"Did she cry?"

"Why would she cry? No, she didn't cry."

"What did she do?"

"She smiled when I gave her the money."

Édouard laughed as he unrolled a sheet of paper he held in his hand. It was a pencil sketch of Clarissa lying on a bed, naked, with a small dog licking her face.

"I spent the time sketching her," Édouard said. "She has the most sensual cheekbones."

"I thought you wanted to take her to bed," Julian said.

"I saw her lying on the bed with the sunlight shining on her through the open window, and I had to capture her on paper."

The next day, Édouard went back to see Clarissa. He spent the afternoon with her and then met Julian that evening at a nearby bar.

"So, did you sleep with her?" Julian asked.

"That's something a gentleman doesn't talk about."

"You're not going to tell me?"

"Use your imagination. But right now, we should get back to the ship."

Julian kept questioning him, but Édouard refused to say if he slept with the girl. He looked at Julian with a self-assured grin. It reminded Julian that he was not as self-assured as Édouard.

Part of Édouard's self-assuredness came from his family's status, Julian thought; his father was a judge, and his mother was the daughter of a French diplomat in Sweden. Julian's status was humble. His father was an army officer, and his mother was a seamstress.

Yet after hearing one particular story from Édouard about his father, Julian considered himself fortunate. Édouard told Julian how he got into a fight with his father when he was fourteen years old. It was his mother's thirty-fifth birthday. Édouard had just come home from school. His father, who was sitting in the living room, jumped up and grabbed Édouard by the neck. He shouted at Édouard, asking him where he had been. "You don't come home some nights because you're in bed with one of your mistresses," Édouard blurted. When his father heard him say that, he pushed Édouard up against a wall and hit him with a clenched fist that bloodied his nose. His mother shouted for them to stop. Édouard hit his father back, but he didn't want to fight him, so he left, only to come back a couple of hours later.

For weeks, he and his father didn't speak to each other. When Julian heard the story, he asked Édouard if he ever wanted to get even with his father. Édouard said that was something he hadn't thought about.

Julian said he couldn't imagine getting into a fight with his father. He was proud of his father, who had slowly moved up the ranks as an army officer. His mother worshiped Julian's father, and they spent time together going for walks.

On their walk back to the port in Rio, the sky turned dark and then suddenly, they heard yelling.

A tall, muscular, dark-skinned boy, probably around fifteen years old, was running with long strides down the road, chased by a white man much bigger than him. The white man weighed at least 300 pounds, while the boy was probably less than 150 pounds. Despite his massive weight, the white man was less than twenty yards behind the boy. He was waving a machete and yelling something in Portuguese.

"He needs our help," Édouard said loudly.

"Who?"

"The boy."

"What can we do?"

"You'll see."

The boy dashed by Édouard and Julian, who were amazed at how fast he could run. The boy kept running, looking back over his shoulder. Maybe the boy didn't need any help, Julian thought. Just as the man ran by them, Édouard jumped him from behind, grabbed the machete, and wrestled the man to the ground. The man got up and was ready to fight Édouard. Sweat was running down his face and he was breathing through clenched teeth. But he raised his fists and began to shout at them.

Édouard stepped back and heaved the machete into some bushes. The man chased after the Machete.

"That will give us more time to get to the boat," Édouard said.

"How did you know to heave the machete?" Julian said as he and Édouard ran toward the boat tied at the end of the dock twenty yards away.

"When you're in trouble, decide in a moment what you need to do."

When they reached the end of the dock, Julian and Édouard jumped into the boat and rowed as fast as they could toward the ship. They looked back at the man. By then, he had found his machete, but all he could do was wave it in the air and keep shouting.

Chapter Four

When Julian Mercier and Édouard Manet returned to Paris, they took the Naval Academy exam and failed it a second time. Neither had any intention of passing it Edouard continued to plead with his father to let him study to become a painter. He showed his father the sketches he did at sea and some paintings of the masters he copied at the Louvre. After days of trying to persuade his father he could make a good living as a painter, Édouard finally won the argument.

Just as he expected, Julian's father did not argue with him about becoming a writer. It disappointed him that Julian failed the Naval exam, but he wasn't going to stand in the way of his ambitions. Julian reassured his father he could earn a good living as a writer. If he couldn't get hired by one of the many Paris journals, he could still support himself by writing articles and selling them to various publications.

The two friends were seeing changes in their lives; Édouard was now seriously interested in music and Julian had made friends with a writer with whom he worked and shared an apartment.

Édouard and his brother, Eugene, were taking piano lessons from a woman his mother hired. Her name was Suzanne Leenhoff. She was Dutch, twenty-three years old, four years older than Édouard and had been in Paris for about two years.

Julian worked as a proofreader at a journal known for its Republic-leaning politics and the critics who wrote about up-and-coming artists and their work. Each night, Julian stopped to see his father on his way home from work. They had long conversations about the articles Julian proofread that day.

One evening in December, Julian hurried to meet Édouard, who continued to live at his parent's home. As Julian reached the house, he was so cold that a biting chill ran down his back. He stood shivering, waiting for Édouard to come to the door.

When Édouard opened the door, he rushed into the main room. Julian noticed the draped curtains that covered a massive window in the main room. The drapes flowed down from the ceiling to the floor, looking much like the curtains of an opera house. The room's walls were covered with decorative blue wallpaper. Circles of small white flowers floated throughout the wallpaper. Julian thought to himself, this was Édouard's father's house, the home of a judge who slept with prostitutes.

Édouard walked over to Julian. "I'd like to introduce you to Suzanne," Édouard said, sounding a little formal and looking toward the center of the room, where a young woman sat at a grand piano.

Suzanne stood up and smiled. "So, you're Julian," she said softly. "Édouard has told me a lot about you."

Édouard's brother, Eugene, was sitting on a chair in the corner of the room. He quickly got up to give the chair to Julian.

"Please take it," Eugene said. "I've been sitting too long today."

Julian noticed how much Eugene sounded and looked like Édouard. Julian had no brothers and wondered what it would be like to have one like Eugene, one who looked and sounded like him.

"Édouard tells me you're thinking about law school," Julian said to Eugene.

"I'm thinking about it."

"Eugene's also interested in painting, but I don't think he's that passionate about it," Édouard said. "But as you can guess, our father wants him to go to law school."

"Is your father home?" Julian asked. "I'd like to say good evening to him."

"No. He's not here tonight," Édouard said quickly, his voice trailing off.

"Nobody's as passionate about painting as Édouard," Suanne said. "I like that about him."

For a moment, Julian looked intensely at Suzanne. Édouard told him she was elegant and beautiful. But Julian didn't see her that way. She was typical of many Dutch women. To be kind, she wasn't beautiful. He was surprised at how large a woman she was and wondered why Édouard thought she was so beautiful, thinking about the other women Édouard had known.

Julian looked up to see Édouard's mother stroll into the room. It was a stroll, Julian thought, just as Édouard had described during their voyage to Rio. Édouard had talked a great deal about his mother and less about his father on their trip.

"Bonjour Madame Manet," Julian said, taking her hand.

"Julian Mercier. Édouard often talks about you," Madame Manet said. "You have a new job?"

"That's right. as a proofreader at *Le Express*," Julian said. "Eventually, I hope to become an art critic."

"That's good," Madame Manet said. "Maybe you can write something good about Édouard's paintings."

"I'd like to."

"He'll be famous someday," Madame Manet said. "But for now, he's studying at a studio."

"I know. He's told me he's not completely happy there."

"It's where he should be," she said, "if he wants to become a great artist."

"I don't know what I'm doing there," Édouard said. He had a frown on his face. "When I come into the studio, it's like entering a tomb, and the models are not natural."

"Now don't complain about Monsieur Couture," Madame Manet said, admonishing Édouard. "He is teaching you how to become a great artist."

While Édouard was talking, Suzanne quietly left the room and went to the kitchen. She returned with a plate full of cookies piled an inch deep.

"Won't you try one?" Suzanne said to Julian.

"Suzanne's a wonderful cook," Madame Manet said. "Don't you think so, Édouard?"

"There's no mistake about that."

Julian thought about Clarissa in Rio, who Édouard said was not a good cook, but that didn't matter. Édouard had been with Clarissa more than a dozen times during their four months in Rio, and each time Julian felt a little jealous. The thought faded when he heard Madam Manet ask him, "So, what does a writer read?"

"I'm sure that many read novels. That's what I read. I just finished a great novel about three musketeers and I wished I'd written it," Julian said, pleased he spoke without stuttering.

His words hung in the air and then there was the sound of gunfire, the clamor of horses, and the beating of drums coming from the street.

"What's going on?" Julian said to Édouard.

Chapter Five

Édouard and Julian grabbed their coats and dashed from the house into the street. A harsh wind whipped around them as they bundled up.

"Let's find out what's going on," Julian said.

They walked quickly along Rue Drouot and heard rifle shots. When they reached the Rue Lafitte, the street of the art dealers, a cloud of smoke and the smell of gunpowder filled the air. As many as a dozen horsemen galloped by them as they watched a group of nine or ten people disburse and run in every direction.

"We've got to get out of here," Édouard shouted.

"I know. Where can we go?"

Through the smoke, Édouard watched a tiny man come out of one shop and run toward them. Édouard recognized him immediately. It was Adolphe Beugniet, a picture dealer whose shop Édouard often visited.

"Monsieur Beugniet," Édouard shouted.

"Come on. Get in here," Beugniet yelled.

The three men hurried into the shop. Huddled in the back, they peered out at the street through a front window. They watched as several shells exploded in the street. When the shelling stopped, Édouard introduced Julian to Monsieur Beugniet.

"I'm more than glad to meet you Monsieur Beugniet," Julian said. "You risked your life for us."

"I wasn't sure if it was Édouard I saw out there," Monsieur

Beugniet said, "but I thought it was probably him. He's come into my shop many times often just to look at Gustave Courbet's paintings."

"Yes, "Julian said. "That's right. Édouard has often talked about Courbet. He told me Courbet won a gold medal from the Salon."

"That's true. Édouard like many aspiring artists would like to win a gold medal from the Salon so, his paintings would not be rejected," Monsieur Beugniet said.

"You're right. Winning the medal would mean my paintings would not be rejected by the Salon," Édouard said. "But right now, that's not important. What is important is what's going on in the streets. Monsieur Beugniet, do you know what's this shelling all about?"

"It's all because of Louis-Napoleon," Beugniet said. "I heard talk he was going to stage a coup because he was upset with the Assembly. It wouldn't let him have another term as president. That's why some think he was going to stage a coup. In fact, he wants to be crowned emperor."

"Do you believe that?" Julian asked.

"Right now, the police and the military are going around the city arresting legislators who were against extending his term and they're also going after those who believe in the Republic and don't want a monarchy, "Beugniet said.

When the shelling had stopped and it had been quiet for over an hour, Édouard said it was time to go. He reached to shake Monsieur's Beugniet's hand. "Thank you. I will never forget what you did for us," Édouard said.

As they left the shop and began their walk home, Édouard took out a pouch of tobacco and a paper from his jacket pocket and began to roll a cigarette. They hadn't been walking more

39

than twenty minutes when Julian spotted five men in uniforms. He thought they were police or a military patrol. One of them, a heavy-set man with a huge double chin, closed in on them and grabbed Édouard's arm.

"What are you doing out at this time of night?" the man asked.

"Just walking," Édouard said and then he began to whistle.

"Just walking. Right," the man said.

The men rushed up and surrounded Édouard and Julian. Within a matter of minutes, they marched them into the police station. Inside, the heavy-set man shoved Édouard and Julian into an empty cell.

"Enjoy the rest of your evening," the man said.

"He's a pig,' Julian said, under his breath.

"He sure looks like one," Édouard whispered.

"I'm worried everyone at home is going to be concerned we haven't gotten back," Édouard said.

"There's nothing we can do about that," Julian said.

The next morning, the heavy-set man came to the cell and told Édouard and Julian they could leave. As they rushed out of the police station, Édouard whispered to Julian that he would have liked to punch the fat man in the face.

"I would have enjoyed that," Julian said.

"But then they would have locked us up for a good many years," Édouard said.

As the two men continued down the street, they came to a two-story building. Looking through one window, they could see a printing press.

"This is the place that *Le Express,* the journal I work for, is printed," Julian said. Posted on the front of the building was a two-foot by four-foot placard. Giant red letters the height of the placard explained why they didn't see anyone in the building working.

This business is closed by order of the President, the placard read.

Louis-Napoleon, Julian thought. "That son of a bitch," Julian said. "He can't do this."

"I don't have to tell you, Julian, that he can do that," Édouard said. "He can shut down any business he wants, especially if it prints journals that publish article favoring the Republic and opposing a monarchy."

"It's just not right," Julian said.

"I'm sorry, Julian. I feel the same way," Édouard said, "But there's nothing we can do about it."

They hurried away from the building, walking for another hour. Julian had kept quiet, holding back his anger. When they reached the next street, Julian saw a dozen people fifty yards ahead of them. Several soldiers forced them to line up against a wall.

"What the hell is happening?" Julian asked.

"We better keep quiet and go around them," Édouard said.

Édouard and Julian kept quiet as they watched in horror as the soldiers raised their rifles and then, on command, opened fire.

"How can they kill them like that in cold blood?" Julian whispered to Édouard.

"They're Louis-Napoleon's soldiers," Édouard said with a grim look on his face.

"Someone should shoot him.," Julian said. He felt sick and ashamed. There was nothing they could do.

They took another street to avoid the soldiers. For the last hour of their walk back to Édouard's parents' home, they were horrified.

"I just can't stop thinking about what we saw," Julian said.

"Neither can I," Édouard said. "It makes me sick, but I can't get my mind off it."

When they finally reached Édouard's parent's home, they agreed to say nothing about the atrocities that turned their stomach, not to Suzanne, nor Édouard's brother nor his mother.

The next day, Julian and Édouard went to the cemetery in Montmartre. They wanted to find a quiet place and talk about what they saw the day before. But it was the cemetery where many were killed the day before were being laid out. They covered each one up from their feet to their neck with blankets. Only their heads were left uncovered.

The police ordered the people who had come to the cemetery to claim their relatives to file past the dead one by one. Julian stood quietly as he watched Édouard take out a pad he always carried with him and begin sketching the dead. For Julian, the sound of the relatives screaming and crying was unsettling. He covered his ears with his hands to block the horrifying noise.

"Why are you sketching them?" Julian asked, trying to understand what Édouard was doing.

"I don't know why," Édouard said, taking a handkerchief from his coat pocket to dry his eyes.

"Maybe, so I'll never forget."

"We won't ever need a sketch to remember what Louis-Napoleon did to these people," Julian said.

Chapter Six

A year later, on the morning of January 29, 1852, Suzanne, who had gone back to Holland, gave birth to a son, Leon. Édouard said nothing about it to Julian that day, although they were together for almost eight hours at the Louvre. It was not until a few years later, when Édouard was in his late twenties, that he talked about Leon, who he would take for walks at least twice a week through the Batignolles, a neighborhood he treasured for that reason.

That day in January, Édouard was copying a painting by Francois Boucher, "Diana Leaving the Bath." Every day, hundreds of artists came to the Louvre to copy the works of the masters. They needed a permit and had to register which painting they were going to copy. For many artists, the Louvre was an education in classical painting.

As he painted, Julian sat in a chair next to Édouard working at his easel. He watched Édouard using quick brush strokes to get the same milky white skin Boucher had painted.

"Monsieur Boucher was a master of the erotic," Édouard said, as he continued to paint.

"Yes, you could say that."

"He paints to titillate."

"He does."

"Yet his tone is innocent."

"Yes. That's right."

Julian wondered, as he often did, not only what it took to become a brilliant painter, but what it took to become a great writer.

Julian had learned much about writing from the writer with whom he had worked and shared an apartment. He looked up to him as a mentor. But the *Le Express* closed its doors, after Louis-Napoleon shut down the business that printed the journal, and dozens of people, including him and his mentor lost their jobs. Julian found another job at a Paris journal, but his mentor had to go to work for a newspaper in Lyon, 400 miles away. Angry he had to move into a tiny studio when he couldn't afford to pay the rent for the apartment, Julian despised Louis-Napoleon even more.

Julian looked up from his chair to see Édouard shaking him.

"I don't think you're listening to me," Édouard said.

"Yes, I was, "Julian said.

He watched Édouard lay his palette and brush down on a small wooden table next to the easel and pointed again to Bouchard's painting of Diana.

"A hundred years ago, this painting was shown in the Salon," Édouard said. "And think of it, just this year the Louvre acquired it."

"What do you think life was like for Monsieur Bouchard?" Julian asked, looking directly at Édouard. Was Bouchard as ambitious as Édouard? Was it necessary to have the same ambition as Édouard to be good enough to exhibit at the Louvre? Julian knew he wasn't as ambitious as Édouard but was determined to become a talented writer.

Julian didn't hear Édouard answer his question and asked another one. "What do you think life was like a hundred years ago?" Julian asked.

"Very different. But one thing has remained the same."

"What's that?" Julian asked.

"Every year the Salon exhibits paintings floor to ceiling and on every available inch. If you can't exhibit at the Salon, you will never be a great artist."

"Édouard, don't you know you are a great artist? "Julian asked. "Why is the Salon so important to you?"

"I told you," Édouard said as he became more irritated. "Because it's the Salon that decides who is and who is not a brilliant painter," Édouard said. "It's the only real public venue for artists."

"You're a talented painter, with or without the Salon," Julian said. "The Salon stifles and corrupts the feeling for the great, the beautiful. It is only a picture shop."

Julian looked away from Édouard, knowing he would never win the argument, and caught a glimpse of a tall heavy-set man, with blazing red hair and a red mustache walking toward them.

"I think he must have heard us," Julian said.

"Yes. I overheard you," he said. "I hate to interrupt, but I thought I heard you talking about the Salon."

"Yes, we were, "Édouard said. "Are you a painter?"

"I see you are, but no, I'm not," he said." Let me introduce myself. I'm Felix Nadar, but please call me Nadar." Then, almost in a single breath and without giving Édouard or Julian a chance to say a word, Nadar introduced himself. "I'm a writer, a journalist, an illustrator, and a master caricaturist. I'm also a daredevil, sometimes reckless, and always irreconcilably opposed to any sign of law and order."

"You don't say?" Édouard responded. "Why don't you catch your breath while I tell you my name? It's Édouard Manet."

"Very good name," Nadar said.

"And I'm Julian Mercier," Julian blurted out.

"Are you a painter too?" Nadar asked Julian.

"No. I'm a writer," Julian said." He was struck not only by Nadar's demeanor but also by his booming baritone voice. He could have a leading role in an opera and was as talkative as a magpie, Julian thought.

"Why did you become a writer?" Nadar asked.

Almost surprised, Julian answered, "I'm a writer because writing keeps my mind going. It never stops."

"There are some people who say writers have something wrong with them," Nadar said. "Some people say writers can be very self-centered. Of course, some people say the same thing about painters."

"They couldn't say that about me," Julian responded.

"Nor could they say it about me," Édouard said. "Who are the people that say that?"

"Who cares what people say?" Nadar said. "I never do. And by the way, your painting is very good."

"Thank you," Édouard said. "Do you spend much time at the Louvre watching people paint?"

"I used to, but this is my first visit in four years."

"Why so long?"

"I just got back from Poland," Nadar said.

"From Poland?" Julian said.

"Yes. My brother Adrien and I signed up as volunteers to help liberate Poland in their fight against Russia. Once in Poland, they arrested us and forced us to work in the coal mines until we escaped several months later and we could get back to Paris."

"That must have been terrible," Julian said.

"It was, but enough about me," Nadar said. "What do you think of Diana?" he asked Julian.

"She's a goddess."

"And not prudish either," Édouard said.

Julian wanted to know more about why Nadar went to Poland. "What makes one choose a political side?" he asked without hesitation, not giving any thought to his chance of stuttering and wanting to learn more from Nadar.

"Knowing the difference between right and wrong," Édouard said. "But knowing what's right is not as easy as it sounds."

"I like your answer," Nadar said. "But it wasn't difficult for me. It was the Polish people's country and not the Russians."

Julian started to speak, but Nadar waved a hand. "Enough of politics and of pondering Diana's virtues. Although I agree with you, Julian, she is a goddess."

"You have good taste," Édouard said.

Felix reached his arm deep into his coat pocket, pulled out a bottle of wine, and laughed.

"Let's go," he said.

"How'd you do that?" Julian asked.

"I have deep pockets," Nadar said, laughing again.

Édouard picked up his canvas. Julian grabbed the easel, the paintbox, and the brushes, and they left the Louvre.

As they walked along the Rue de Rivoli, Nadar did most of the talking, about people he knew, and there were many, about Paris, and the things he had accomplished, including writing a novel.

Julian thought nothing could be better than listening to someone like Nadar. This is what he'd always imagined the artistic life was like. Nadar walked quickly and kept on talking, letting Édouard and Julian join in on the conversation every once in a while. Édouard kept up with Nadar because of his jaunty stride. He walked with his head thrown back and chin up in the air listening to the dry pavement echo under his feet. Julian was determined to keep up with them so he could hear every word

Nadar said and did for nearly an hour before Nadar announced he was hungry.

"There's a woman I know who has the best oysters," Nadar said. "They taste so good; you'll think you've gone to heaven."

"Let's go. That sounds good to me," Julian said. They walked a few minutes more, stopping in front of a woman shucking oysters. She looked like many of the women who shucked oysters, old and tired. But there was something about her that set her apart from the other women of her trade; it was a dark brown mustache that floated above her upper lip.

"It's not good to stare," Nadar said to Édouard, who seemed to be focused on the woman's face.

"I'm not staring at her," Édouard said. "I thought she'd make an interesting subject for a painting."

"Maybe she would," Nadar said. "But for now, let's get some of her oysters. "They come fresh every day from off the coast of Normandy."

A smile appeared on the woman's lips as she began opening oysters for Nadar. There was a grace about the way she opened them, slow and methodical, sliding the knife clutched in her hand between the shells. Julian looked at Nadar, who was less graceful, gulping down one oyster after another.

The woman opened several oysters for Julian and Édouard. But they couldn't catch up with Nadar, who made a show of stuffing himself, while growing a mound of shells piled up at their feet.

"Who's going to pick up the shells?" Julian asked.

"Don't worry. She will," Nadar said, as he watched Édouard delicately swallow another oyster.

"Édouard, you are too serious," Nadar said. He reached down for the bottle of wine he had placed on the ground. "Drink some more," he said, handing the bottle to Édouard, who took a swig.

"I think I've had enough wine and oysters." He gave the bottle back to Nadar, reached into his coat pocket and pulled out several francs to pay the woman for the oysters.

"Here is an extra two francs," Édouard said.

"That's not enough," Nadar said, handing the woman two more francs.

"Thank you, sirs," the woman said, taking a cloth she had in her pocket and wiping her mustache, which had become moist.

"Wait a minute," Julian said to the woman. He told Édouard he didn't have any money and asked him for three francs, which he gave to the woman.

"Thank you too, sir," she said, her smile widening."

The three friends caught a carriage to return to their homes.

"It's been a good evening," Nadar said.

"Yes, it has," Julian said, thinking about all the wine they drank and eating so many oysters with Édouard and Nadar, someone who might become another good friend.

Chapter Seven

In the spring of 1856, Édouard, his brother Eugene, and Julian traveled by train to Florence. After they arrived and checked into a hotel, they grabbed a carriage to the Uffizi Gallery. Eugene carried Édouard's easel and canvas, and Julian brought the bag with the paints and palette.

Once they got to the gallery, they hurried to where Titian's "Venus de Urbino" hung, a young woman, nude, the goddess Venus, reclining on a couch in lavish palace surroundings.

Eugene and Julian stood quietly, watching Édouard's as he gazed at the painting. Édouard's eyes were fixed on the massive painting, almost four feet high and over five feet wide.

The flow of light filled Édouard with enthusiasm. "It's stunning."

Édouard grabbed the easel from Eugene and set it up just a few feet from Titian's Venus. He quickly placed the empty canvas Eugene handed to him on the easel. Julian opened the box of paints and gave them to Édouard. After he mixed his paints on the pallet, Édouard began to paint his Venus.

Several days before coming to Florence, they had been in Rome, where Édouard spent hours copying Titian's "Sacred and Profane Love" at the Galleria Borghese. Julian wondered how much time Édouard would spend painting his Venus, although he didn't care how long because Titian was one of Édouard's favorite artists.

"What do you think?" Édouard asked Eugene, his voice was

full of emotion.

"It's just incredible."

"It's heroic," Julian said, jumping into the conversation. "As much as Homer's *Odyssey*," he said, sitting down on the floor, placing his hand under his chin, admiring the painting. "Did you know he painted it for the Duke of Urbino? I think around 1540?" Julian said. "It's been hanging in the Uffizi since 1730."

"You're quite the classicist and art historian," Édouard said.

Édouard and Eugene looked pensively at Julian, who thought they were trying to stare him down and get him to be quiet.

"They called Titian a sun among the stars," Julian said. "He was the most versatile of all his contemporaries, often painting with loose brushwork."

"How do you know so much about Titian?" Édouard asked.

"What? Are you surprised?"

"Yes. But there's one thing about Titian I bet you didn't know."

"What?"

"His younger brother was also a painter," Édouard said, looking at Eugene.

"I knew that," Julian said.

"I did too," Eugene said. "Besides having a brother who was a painter, Titian was one of the first artists to use living, breathing women for models, like you, Édouard."

Édouard ignored the compliment. "There's something you could do for me," Édouard said.

"What's that?"

"I'd like you to take your painting as seriously as your knowledge of Titian."

"I know, and there are times I think about it."

51

"You need to do more than think about it."

"Let's not talk any more about it right now," Eugene said.

"All right, but I want you to think about it."

Why was Édouard coming down so hard on Eugene to become a painter, Julian wondered. Was it vengeance, although Édouard had said he was not capable of it? Why wouldn't Édouard try to get even with his father for all the years he was pushed to become something other than a painter? What if he fought with his father about becoming a writer as much as Édouard did with his father to become a painter? Would that help make him as ambitious as Édouard? No, he wouldn't trade his relationship with his father for one that helped shape Édouard's life.

Julian returned to watching Édouard paint. Édouard had been at it for several hours when he stopped and pulled out his pocket watch to look at the time.

"We've been here long enough," Édouard said. "I'm satisfied with what I've done. Let's go back to the hotel. I'll finish it when we return to Paris."

When Édouard said he was ready to go, they left the gallery and got a carriage back to their hotel. There was a small café on the first floor of the hotel, where they found an open table to have dinner. It was a small marble table decorated at the center with a crystal vase full of wildflowers.

"This reminds me of Paris," Julian said.

"This isn't Paris," Édouard said. "Just listen to the people around us."

"The cafe owner came over to their table, introduced himself, and took their orders.

"He spoke in French," Julian said.

"Yes, he did. Many people here can speak French," Édouard

said. "But he has an Austrian accent, not like someone from Florence."

"I think you're right," Julian said.

"He is," Eugene chimed in.

"Let me explain why he has an Austrian accent, "Édouard said. "Austria rules Florence."

"Yes, I know," Julian said.

"But there will come a day," Édouard said, "when the people of Florence will rise up and take back their homeland."

As Édouard continued to talk, Julian noticed a man sitting at a table a few feet away. He got up quickly and sauntered over to their table. The man also spoke French with an Austrian accent.

"Did I hear you right?" the man asked Édouard.

"What do you mean?" Édouard said.

"That the people of Florence will rise up and take back their country from Austria," the man said.

"That's what he said," Eugene responded. "Why? Does that bother you?"

Before Eugene finished speaking, the man reached into his coat, pulled out a glove, and struck Édouard in the face with it.

"I challenge you to a duel," the man said.

"We don't duel with Austrians," Eugene said. "We stand up and fight them."

Édouard jumped up and knocked the man down with one punch. The man was sprawled out on the floor and wasn't moving. Blood was oozing from the man's mouth. Julian watched the café owner, who had just returned, bend down to check the man's pulse.

"Is he all right?" Julian asked the café owner. He thought by showing concern for the man the café owner wouldn't think they were responsible for him being out cold on the floor.

"I think so," the café owner said. "What happened here?" he

asked.

"I don't know," Édouard said. "Maybe it was something he ate."

"I don't think so," the café owner said with a nasty look on his face.

"You can't be too sure," Eugene said, handing the café owner money to cover the bill.

Within minutes, the three hurried upstairs to their hotel room and packed their bags. Édouard paid the hotel bill while Eugene and Julian carried the bags to a carriage waiting outside.

"Take us to the train station," Julian said as they jumped into the carriage.

Minutes later, after the carriage had gone less than a few hundred yards, Julian looked back to see the café owner shouting and running after them.

"Can't you make this carriage go any faster?" Julian asked the driver. "We'll miss our train, if you don't."

"I'll try," the driver said, cracking the whip in his hand several times, spurring the horses into a gallop. They quickly put enough distance between the café owner and the carriage so he wouldn't be able to catch up with them.

When they arrived at the train station, they got out of the carriage and looked at each other.

"What do you think?" Édouard said, putting his hand on Julian's shoulder.

"I guess the man you knocked down told the café owner what had happened," Julian said.

"No. I mean what do you think about Florence being under the thumb of Austria? You didn't say anything about it back at the café," Édouard said.

"You didn't give me a chance to say anything," Julian said. "What I would have said is that I'm proud of what you did.

Someone needed to do it."

"Oh," Édouard said.

"I thought you knew me better," Julian said. He had a frustrated look on his face. "No country has the right to invade or rule another.

Chapter Eight

It was a brisk fall day two years later, November 1858, as Édouard and Julian walked the streets of central Paris, searching for a man to be the subject of Édouard's next painting, "The Absinthe Drinker".

"He's going to have to be someone who's broken, someone who represents Paris' downtrodden, a lowlife, an alcoholic, but he also must have an arresting presence. That's why I'm looking for the perfect ragpicker."

After an hour of scouting the streets, they came across a wrinkled old man. Julian greeted him but he was silent. His mouth was twisted, and Julian thought the deformity prevented him from speaking. It was a good feeling knowing he didn't have to live with the old man's deformity. His stammering, which was becoming less of a problem, was much easier to accept.

The old man was a public writer who earned a living by writing letters and documents for those who couldn't write. He was sitting in a booth with a pen in hand, writing something for a young boy standing over him. Julian moved closer and saw it was a poem from a boy to a young girl.

"He doesn't have to open his mouth to speak," Julian said, looking at Édouard. "What he writes gives him a voice."

"I couldn't agree more," Édouard said. "But there're going to be fewer and fewer of them around," Édouard said. "The old man's job is going away. More and more people are learning to read and write. It's happening at the same time Paris is changing when many of its neighborhoods are being demolished and rebuilt."

Much of Paris for years was hideous with its open sewers and narrow streets. The span between the Louvre and the courtyard of the Tuileries Palace was nasty and foul. Beyond the Carrousel Bridge, there were crumbling houses, and many of the structures, the stores, and the shops were squeezed together.

"The crowded, unhealthy neighborhoods are being demolished," Édouard said. "The avenues are being widened and parks are being created. This is going to be a painter's dream."

"Writers are going to capture the new Paris, but they are also going to write about what's been lost."

"There are some things that are not going to change. Despite what is changing, there will always be ragpickers."

"I'm not so sure."

"The ragpicker is vital to everyday life. How can you replace someone who picks up and sells what's been thrown away?"

"They're a necessary evil?"

"I would say they're necessary."

Édouard had heard about one ragpicker who frequented the neighborhood around the Louvre. As Édouard and Julian strolled the area, a man wrapped in a brown opera cloak stumbled from out of the shadows and stood in front of them.

The smell of licorice floated in the air, suggesting he must have had a few glasses of absinthe and could be drunk, but he was just the subject Édouard wanted, Julian thought.

"Have you had a good night?" Édouard asked, slurring his syllables so that he would sound more like a common Parisian than the twenty-seven-year-old son of a judge. But Édouard couldn't conceal his heritage.

"Yes. I've got some glass that can be melted down and a few

bones that can be turned into pigment," the ragpicker said. "That means money for me."

"You've probably picked enough to pay for a few drinks tonight," Édouard said.

"And then some."

"But don't you ever tire of being a ferret?"

"What did you say?"

"I said, don't you get tired of being a ferret?"

The ragpicker turned toward Édouard, revealing the right side of his face. A scar ran from his ear to the corner of his mouth.

Édouard's eyes focused on the scar. "Don't I know you?" Édouard asked. He remembered the scar on the sailor who attacked Julian and him on the *Le Havre et Guadeloupe*.

"Why the hell did you call me a ferret?"

The ragpicker reached into his pocket and pulled out a knife. The handle glimmered under the streetlamp. It looked like the one the sailor had pulled on Julian and Édouard eleven years earlier. It had the same gold star embedded in the pearl handle.

"Put it away," Édouard demanded.

"You can't tell me what to do," the ragpicker said, slurring his words. "I'll put the knife away if, and only if, you apologize."

"Apologize for what?" Édouard said.

"For calling me a ferret."

Julian looked more closely at the ragpicker, who was having trouble keeping his balance. He saw the scar on the ragpicker's face and the knife was vaguely familiar. Julian was almost sure he was the sailor who wanted to kill him and Édouard on the ship to Rio.

"Put the knife away," Édouard demanded again.

The ragpicker lifted his cloak and reached into the pocket in his ragged trousers with the knife in his hand and put it away.

"What's your name?" Édouard asked.

"Pelleton. Pierre Pelleton. What's it to you?"

Édouard remembered Pelleton was the name of the sailor who attacked him and Julian ten years before.

"Do you remember me?" Édouard asked."

The ragpicker stared at Édouard for a moment before speaking. "Yes. I think I do. Weren't you on that ship? You got me in trouble with the captain."

"I don't remember you returning to Paris on the ship," Édouard said.

"I didn't, not for another three years."

"Why not?"

"It's too long a story. Why are you asking?"

"Never mind. It doesn't matter right now."

Julian was interested in knowing why Pierre didn't return to Paris on the ship. Had he tried to kill someone else?

Édouard stepped closer to Pierre. "I have a proposition for you," Édouard said.

"What is it"?

"I want to make you an offer."

"For what?"

"I want you to sit for me for a painting."

"What's in it for me?"

"I'll pay you well."

"How much? You need to make it worth my while."

"Two francs a sitting, and you'll have a carriage to take you back and forth to my studio."

"That's not enough."

"That's enough to pay for a good meal each time you sit."

"I said it's not enough."

"All right. Four francs for each sitting and, of course, money for the carriage."

"What do you pay others?"

"I've made you an excellent offer. You can take it or leave it."

The ragpicker was silent for a moment and then looked up at Édouard. "Okay. We have a deal," he said.

"Good. You can start tomorrow, "Édouard said, handing him his card. "Here's the address. You need to be at my studio at noon. I'm giving enough for the carriage. I want you to be at my studio on time at noon."

Chapter Nine

Julian arrived at the studio a few minutes before noon and Pierre got there a half an hour later. Édouard was mixing his paints from the tubes onto a palette when Pierre arrived. He put down the palette when he heard a knock on the door and went to open it.

"Good morning, Pierre," Édouard said.

"Do you always say good morning?" Pierre asked.

"It's good manners."

"Then, good morning. You're certainly well dressed," Pierre said, as he walked into the studio.

"Why do you say that? This is how I always dress." He looked at what he was wearing, the jacket squeezed at the waist, a loose-fitted linen shirt, and light-colored trousers.

"I see your gloves and hat are on the table over there."

"If I go out to a café later in the day, I have my gloves and hat handy."

"I didn't mean to offend you."

"You didn't. I see you had no trouble getting here."

"It was easy enough. The driver knew the address. He said he had picked up a man from this address who he thought was a painter."

"That's good to hear. Maybe I can make you famous."

Édouard began to lift a huge three-by-four-foot canvas onto the easel in the center of the studio. Julian had gotten up to help when Alexandre, Édouard 's thirteen-year-old assistant, who had been sweeping the studio, put his broom aside and rushed over to grab one end of the canvas.

"I'll help," Alexandre said. "I can do it." Alexandre almost always had a smile on his face. It was a smile that concealed where he came from. His mother and father were so poor they couldn't afford to take care of him. Édouard and Julian found him on the street dressed in rags and begging for food. Édouard took him in immediately.

"That's good, Alexandre. Thanks for your help," Édouard said. "You can go back to sweeping now."

Édouard straightened the canvas on the easel. "Stand over there," Édouard said to Pierre, as he pointed to the center of the studio.

"Is this what you want?"

"Yes, that's fine. I paint what I see."

Édouard began by blocking out the figure of the man. When he applied the paint, he brushed wet layers of paint on existing layers. His brush strokes were broad, quick, and loose, visible rather than delicately blended and invisible. He painted in brown then gray and then black tones on the gigantic canvas. Every few moments, he would look up at Pierre.

"I've wanted to ask you," Julian said, looking at Pierre. "Why didn't you return to Le Havre with the ship?"

"It's a long story, but I'll take the time to tell you if Édouard doesn't mind me talking while he's painting me."

"Go ahead, I don't mind. I've been wondering myself."

"I met a woman who came up to me when I was walking around the city. She was friendly enough and so I went home with her. But she didn't tell me she had a husband."

"So, what happened?" Julian asked.

"The husband broke down the door and came crashing in. He saw us in the bed together. Before I could run, there was a pistol pointed at me." "What did you do?" Édouard asked as he put down his brush and stopped painting to listen.

"I grabbed his arm and tried to wrestle the pistol away from him, but it went off, and the next thing I knew, his wife was lying on the floor in a pool of blood."

"Was she dead?" Édouard asked.

"She looked dead. I stood looking at her with the gun in my hand. A few minutes later, the police arrived."

Alexandre, who was listening, had grabbed a piece of candy from a box on the table in the corner of the room. Julian watched him stuff the candy into his mouth. It was the size of a five-franc coin and Alexandre had a smile on his face.

"You're supposed to ask," Édouard said.

Alexandre moved slowly away from the table and his smile disappeared.

"He's earned it, Édouard," Julian said.

"Go ahead, you can have it," Édouard said to Alexandre and then turned to Pierre.

"What happened when the police arrived?"

"I wound up going to prison."

Édouard continued to ask questions. "How long were you in prison?"

"Eighteen months," Pierre said.

For Julian, none of Pierre's words revealed any remorse for the woman's death. Was he a man without a conscience?

"But after a few months, I wished I was dead. We were starving, and the guards beat us almost every day."

"So, they let you out of prison after just eighteen months? "Julian asked.

"No. I knew the only way to get out of that lousy prison was to escape."

"So, you escaped?"

"We did. One night, I and two other prisoners overtook the guard on duty. I twisted his neck and he fell to the ground like a sack of potatoes. Then we ran for our lives."

Édouard and Julian listened with their eyes wide open, while Alexandre stared at Pierre. "A few days later, I stowed away on a ship back to France. I couldn't find work in Paris so that's when my days as a ragpicker began."

"And now you're here and I need you to come every day until I finish the painting. Can you do that?"

"Yes, as long as you keep paying me."

Pierre arrived every day precisely at noon for the next six weeks until the painting was finished. On the day Édouard completed it and for most of the other days, Julian sat listening to Pierre's stories and following the painting's progress until the painting was finished.

"I'm sure the Salon's going to accept it," Julian said to Édouard.

"We'll have to see," Édouard said, as he walked over to Pierre and gave him ten extra francs.

Pierre reached out to shake Édouard's hand. "I hope it's accepted by the Salon," Pierre said. "What do I get if it is?"

"You'll be famous. That's what you get." Julian said.

"I'm learning what you really think of me. You can't fool me anymore. You despise me because of what happened on the ship."

"It was a long time ago. I don't know what I think about you."

"Enough," Édouard said, walking Pierre to the door.

The street was busy with carriages going in both directions. Pierre was staring at the ten francs in his hand when Édouard saw a carriage without a driver racing down the street. It was coming toward Pierre. "Watch out," Édouard shouted at Pierre as he rushed to pull him back from the street, scarcely avoiding the oncoming carriage.

"You saved my life," Pierre said, shaking.

"Next time, watch where you're going," Edouard said, helping Pierre get into the next carriage.

The following day, Édouard began work on another painting, "Boy with Cherries." Alexandre modeled for the painting. Before he began to pose for it, Alexandre reached for a piece of candy. Julian watched Édouard reprimand Alexandre for not asking.

"Every time," Édouard said. "He doesn't listen, and he doesn't appreciate what I've done for him."

"He's just a boy," Julian said. "You need to understand that."

For the next few weeks, Julian watched as Édouard worked on the painting. But Édouard wouldn't talk to the boy.

Several days later, after leaving Alexandre to clean up the studio, they returned from lunch. The boy was dangling from a rope he had attached to an armoire.

"Why did he do this?" Édouard screamed. He had tears in his eyes.

"You can't blame yourself," Julian said. He couldn't remember if he had ever seen Édouard cry.

"You didn't know he'd do something like this."

"I should have. I knew he looked up to me," Édouard said." I should have treated him much better."

They both stood silent for a moment, looking at the lifeless boy.

"We've got to get him down," Julian said, his voice shaking.

Édouard gazed at the boy. His feet were almost touching the floor, his face puffed up, and his eyes still open. Julian supported the boy's body and Édouard cut the rope and laid him down on a sofa.

"I'll carry this with me for the rest of my life," Édouard said, his voice breaking.

A few days later, Édouard told Julian he could no longer work from that studio. He moved to another one and rented a nearby apartment. Édouard immersed himself in his painting, trying to forget about the boy's death. For more than two months, after the boy's suicide, when Édouard would go to the café with Julian, he would often ask, "Why did I scold him?"

"Maybe you were too strict with him like your father was with you. But it wasn't your fault," Julian told him many times. Julian was angry with how Édouard treated the boy, but he never told him how angry he was. A good friend wouldn't.

Chapter Ten

For months after Pierre finished sitting for "The Absinthe Drinker" he spent hours at Édouard's studio. He told Édouard about the Paris he knew, the dangerous class, the vagabonds and the beggars, the ragpickers, and the prostitutes; the spine of Paris street life. He talked without interruption, while Édouard painted.

Pierre also became a fixture at the Café Guerbois. The three of them often frequented it in the evening. Any bad feelings Julian and Pierre had against each other they brushed aside.

When they walked into the café, Édouard seemed to enjoy the looks Pierre got from some of the fashionable café patrons. Pierre sometimes got a second look, maintaining his appearance as a ragpicker, while Édouard, with his top hat and waistcoat, was never ignored.

One evening in March 1859, before they left for the café, Édouard Julian and Pierre had some news he was going to announce. Julian thought it might be about whether the Salon accepted Edouard's painting, "The Absinthe Drinker."

"What's it about?" Julian asked.

"I'll tell you when we're at the café."

"You can't tell us now?" Julian asked, throwing his hands up in the air.

"No. I'm sure you can wait."

When they arrived at the café, it was crowded with writers and artists. Édouard walked over to the table where Nadar and Charles Baudelaire, the poet and a close friend, were sitting.

"May we join you?" Édouard asked.

"Of course," Nadar said.

Julian and Pierre sat down at the table while Édouard stood.

"You're all my friends here, and I know you've been wondering whether the Salon would accept or reject my painting, "The Absinthe Drinking."

"Yes, what about it?" Baudelaire asked.

"I have to tell you it was rejected. There was only one vote in favor and that was Eugene Delacroix."

"He was the only great painter among them," Baudelaire said.

"But one is not enough," Édouard said.

Julian was silent, angry that Édouard didn't share the news with him first. A friend would have.

"Why did they reject it?" Nadar asked.

"They said a drunk was offensive."

"They're all around us," Baudelaire said with a smile.

"They didn't like my technique. They said it was too loose and it lacked definition."

"Don't listen to them," Baudelaire said. "You've got to be true."

"That's why they rejected it," Édouard said. "I was true."

Nadar sat quietly for a moment, gathering his thoughts. "These institutions sometimes have a hard time understanding what is new," Nadar said. "It's like teaching the theory of photography. You can teach theory in an hour. What can't be taught are the nuances that make it an art."

"It's too bad the jury doesn't think the way you do," Édouard said.

Pierre looked up from his drink. "They don't know a damn thing about art," he said. "We should do something about it."

"What do you propose?" Nadar asked.

"I don't know, but something," Pierre said.

"There's got to be a way for new artists to exhibit their work," Nadar said.

Édouard looked frustrated and got up from the table." I don't want to talk about it anymore," he said, rushing out of the café.

"He's an exceptional talent," Baudelaire said, watching Édouard leave the café. "But his character sometimes is weak. He can be crushed and shocked by things that should be expected."

"What do you mean, expected?" Nadar asked.

"He knows better than anyone his work is different from the art that the Salon accepts."

"Like your poetry, Charles," Nadar said.

"I know it too well," Baudelaire said, as he motioned to a waiter to bring him another glass of wine.

An hour later, Édouard returned. He strode into the crowded café with a bloody towel around his hand. Everyone looked up to see him catch himself before he stumbled.

"What are you looking at?" Édouard asked.

"You," Baudelaire said.

"Do you think I slashed my wrist?"

"Yes," Baudelaire said.

"I wouldn't do that. What I did was to shatter a huge glass door banging my fist against it."

"Why?" Nadar asked. 'Why would you do that?'

"To free me of my anger."

Julian walked over to Édouard and took him aside. He looked at the towel around his hand. "Someone should take you home," Julian said. "I know you too well. You always have to put on a show."

"If you were as ambitious as me, you'd know how I felt," Édouard said.

"I think I know," Julian said. He tightened the towel around Édouard 's hand and thought for a moment about twisting it around Édouard 's neck. He was tired of Édouard 's obsession with the Salon. But he dismissed the idea and flagged down a carriage to take Édouard home.

Chapter Eleven

Three years after "The Absinthe Drinker" was rejected by the Salon, in September 1862, Édouard met a new model, Victorine Meurent. Julian and Édouard were walking outside the Palais de Justice when they spotted her in a crowd.

She was unlike most other models. She wasn't stately, voluptuous, or a great beauty. She had a round and expressionless face. She was short and slightly built, with striking red hair and brown eyes.

When Édouard saw her, he was struck by her unique appearance. Trying to get her attention, Édouard and Julian pushed through the crowd.

"Mademoiselle, mademoiselle I need to talk to you," Édouard shouted.

She turned to Édouard. "You don't have to shout at me, sir. I can hear you." She walked briskly with a guitar tucked under her arm.

"Do you play the guitar?" he said, trying to keep up with her.

"I do for money."

"Where? In cafés?"

"Wherever I can. In cafes. On the street."

She stopped walking and stood looking up at Édouard.

"Do you have a name?" Édouard asked.

"Of course, I do."

"What is it?"

"Victorine. What's yours?" she said, glancing over her

shoulder as if she were looking for someone.

It was pouring. Édouard, who often carried an umbrella because of how often it rained, opened it and held it over Victorine. "I'm Édouard Manet. I'm a painter. "

"Are you someone important?"

"Only if you'd like to make some money."

"What do you mean?"

"I'd like to pay you to model for me."

"How do I know I can trust you?"

"Look at us," Julian said. "Do we look like criminals?"

"Who are you?" she asked Julian.

"I'm Édouard 's friend, Julian, and I'm also a writer."

"A painter and a writer. I guess I shouldn't be afraid."

"Let's get a carriage and go to my studio," Édouard said. "We can talk there."

"I don't know if I should go with you."

"You can trust us," Édouard said.

"All right, I'll take a chance."

Édouard quickly got a carriage, and the three of them got in. As the carriage slowly traveled along the Rue de Rivoli, Victorine looked out and back down the street. It was the third time she had looked back.

"What's wrong?" Édouard asked. "Why do you keep looking back? Is someone following you?"

"No. No one is following me."

When they arrived, Victorine climbed down from the carriage before Édouard could help her.

"I can get out myself," she said, hurrying to the door of Édouard 's studio.

"Go right in," Édouard said after opening the door.

Julian went to the fireplace and got a fire going, while Édouard sat down with Victorine on the sofa in one corner of the studio. It was only a matter of minutes before Julian got the fire going and sat down on a chair next to the sofa.

"This is a very large studio," Victorine said, her eyes looking around the room.

The studio had a high ceiling, which helped make it look larger than it was. On the walls, several of Édouard 's paintings hung. There was a table in the middle with a basket of fruit. A stand used for the cups containing paint brushes and palettes stood next to an easel. Aluminum tubes of paint lay next to the cups. The aromatic scent of linseed oil and turpentine permeated the studio.

Édouard got up to close the curtains that draped the window overlooking the street. Victorine had settled back on the sofa.

"So, do you like my studio?" Édouard asked Victorine. "I like a large studio. I think DaVinci was wrong when he said an artist's studio should be a small space."

"Who's DaVinci?" Victorine asked.

"He's an artist who's been dead for three hundred years. He believed small rooms disciplined the mind and large ones distracted from it."

"I like a large studio," Victorine said, laughing. "There's a lot you can do in one."

Victorine kept her eyes on Édouard and seemed captivated by his words. Then, without a moment's notice, she unbuttoned her blouse.

"I better leave," Julian said, acting surprised.

"You don't have to leave," Victorine said. "I'm just going to show my breasts so Édouard will pay me well to model for him."

Julian thought for a moment about how uninhibited she was. The perfect model for Édouard.

She finished unbuttoning her blouse and then took it off. There was nothing underneath the blouse except for her firm, round, perfectly shaped mounds. They stood erect as she caressed them with both her hands.

"Do you like them?"

"Yes," Édouard said. "Very much."

Victorine put her blouse back on. A moment later, Édouard heard a loud banging on the door.

"Who is it?" Édouard shouted.

"I know she's in there," the voice hollered back.

Édouard opened the door, and a skinny, balding man pushed his way into the studio. Édouard wasn't quick enough to stop him.

"What do you want?" Édouard asked.

"She owes me money," the man said, pointing at Victorine.

"For what?"

"She owes me a fare. I took her to the Palais de Justice. She jumped out of the carriage and ran off without paying me."

"Do you owe him money? Is that why you kept looking out the carriage window?"

"Yes. That's the reason."

The man said he had tracked Victorine to the studio and was waiting outside to get the money she owed him. But he got tired of waiting and that's why he barged into the studio.

"How much do you owe him?" Édouard asked.

"Three francs," the driver said.

Édouard reached into his pocket and handed the driver the money. "Here you are. Now, you can go on your way."

The driver took the money and quickly left.

"There's a little larceny in your heart," Édouard said, smiling at Victorine.

"Not always."

"I'll get you a carriage to take you home. Here are some francs to get home and to come back tomorrow. I'll see you at nine in the morning. That's when the light is best."

74

Chapter Twelve

Édouard Manet's Journal
September 5, 1862

She was my aphrodisiac, standing naked in my studio. I wanted her to give herself to me. I wanted to paint her.

She arrived at my studio exactly at nine. I had been told by other painters she posed for that she was always punctual.

She quickly sat down on the couch in the corner of the studio. There was the light from the window across from the couch shining on her face She was simply dressed, wearing a cotton frock with a girlish high neck. A ribbon was awkwardly tied around her neck. The only jewelry she had on was a pair of tiny pearl earnings.

Victorine was open in every way. She told me about herself. She said was eighteen years old and came from a poor working-class family. Her father was an engraver and her mother took in laundry.

Her secret ambition was to become an artist. I told her that was a grand ambition, but that it was hard for a woman to be accepted as an artist.

She was inquisitive. She asked me about my background. I told her about my pompous father, my voyage to Rio, my studies with Thomas Couture, and my ambition to have my art shown at the Louvre.

She got up quietly from the couch and picked up several

Spanish costumes a tailor had made for me. They were in a heap on a chair in the corner of the studio. She asked me about the costumes.

She was intriguing. Victorine. I loved the sound of her name. I loved the sound of her shy voice. I felt warm standing next to her. I reminded myself about my commitment to Suzanne, but I still felt euphoric being alone in the studio with this woman.

I told her I wanted to paint a Spanish matador. I showed her a few photographs I had of a matador. I told Victorine I went through my Spanish period like the rest of Paris. In March, the year before, I told her I had seen Louise Marquet dance the role of the Espada in Graziosa at the Opera. She laughed and said she had never been to the opera. I wondered what it would be like to take her to the opera. But I couldn't do that. I wanted her to give herself to me.

I told her about "The Absinthe Drinker" and how it was rejected by the Salon. I told her how I enjoyed being loved and admired and that women were such wonderful pleasures. I had just met this young woman the day before and I was opening up about my deepest thoughts. I told her my next great painting would be of a naked woman having lunch on the grass with two well-dressed men. I told her I wanted her to model for that painting.

I needed to see her naked Slowly, she pulled off her cotton frock. She had nothing on underneath the frock, no stockings or garters, no chemise, no corset.

She asked me if I liked her body. I told her I did. She smiled and said go ahead, do what you want. I lifted her up in my arms and carried her to the couch. Sitting next to her, close enough to rub her body against mine, I slowly ran her nipples through my fingers. They were firm and warm. I looked into her eyes.

She unbuttoned my shirt. When she had finished taking off my shirt, she reached for my pants and unbuttoned them. I slowly pulled my pants off, exposing my body to hers. I was filled with excitement. She asked me what I wanted to do. I told her I wanted to be in her.

I could not resist her breasts and the warmth between her legs. I kissed every inch of her body and asked her if she liked it. She said yes, go ahead.

Slowly, I entered her. We moved together, up and down. We were both silent, enjoying each other's body.

Chapter Thirteen

Victorine was at Édouard 's studio almost every day posing for his next painting, "Luncheon on the Grass." Julian had gone to Boulogne, a seaport town on the northern coast of France, to work on his novel. Every day Julian watched the people of Boulogne walk along the walls of the town. They seemed mesmerized by the sea and a skyline dominated by the Basilica de Notre Dame. Boulogne also mesmerized him, and he wound up spending the day outside walking around the quaint town.

After a few days there, he realized he was not getting much done on his novel, so he went back to Paris.

The day Julian got back, Édouard invited him to his studio to see the progress of his latest painting. Before Julian had taken off his coat, Édouard asked him about Boulogne and how his novel was coming.

"Slowly and I'm angry with myself for not getting much done there," Julian said.

"I think by being back in Paris, you'll get more done."

"Maybe."

"You said it was about a writer?"

"Yes, about a writer who never finishes what he starts."

"It should be about a writer who finishes everything he begins."

"We'll see," Julian said, as he watched Victorine come into the studio from the next room. She was wrapped in a blanket.

"We've been working hard," Édouard said.

Victorine laughed for a moment. "Yes, we have."

"Isn't it immense?" Édouard asked, pointing to the canvas on the easel next to where he stood "It's more than six feet high and almost nine feet wide."

Julian looked at the painting. Victorine was sitting naked on the ground in the woods having a picnic with two fully dressed men and a scantily dressed woman bather in the distance. "I see," Julian said.

"What do you think? I've been experimenting with canvases," Édouard said, a smile spreading over his face, as Julian looked more closely at the painting. "Instead of using a canvas with a dark undercoat, I'm working with one treated with an off-white primer. It's a painting of an outing and the primer brightens it."

"I like the painting, but doesn't the primer diminish its depth?" Julian asked.

"I'm not interested in illusions. Painting is more than that."

Julian turned away from the painting to watch the blanket around Victorine slide down past her breasts.

Victorine quickly reached down to pull the blanket up. "It's good to see you, Julian. As you can see, I'm having trouble keeping myself covered up. You'll have to excuse me for a minute so I can get dressed," Victorine said, as she walked back into the adjacent room and closed the door.

Julian looked around the studio and noticed it was unusually messy. Paint tubes were scattered around the room. A dozen wilting red roses were bent over in a vase on a corner table and Édouard's frock coat was thrown on a chair.

"I've been working so hard on the painting, I haven't had the time to keep the studio the way it should be," Édouard said, as he grabbed his coat and hung it up in the studio armoire.

"I wouldn't worry about it," Julian said.

"Victorine is the perfect subject for this painting," Édouard said.

"I can see that. Where does she stay at night? Here?"

"No. She's here only during the day."

"I see."

"We do a lot of talking."

"What do you talk about?"

"About everything."

"What do you mean?"

"She likes poetry and understands it. We've talked about Baudelaire's poetry."

"You have?"

"Yes, I gave Victorine a copy of *Les Fleurs du Mal* (Flowers of Evil). I don't need to tell you because you know very well that many people have attacked him and his poetry for being scandalous."

"What does Victorine think of his poetry?" Julian asked.

"She thinks that it is beautiful."

"Are you going to go on seeing her?"

"What do you mean, seeing her?"

"After you've finished the painting you're working on now."

"I'll keep using her as a model. There's something special about her."

"There is?"

"Well, she's not someone I would take home to one of my mother's Thursday night socials, but she is interesting."

Just then, Victorine walked back into the studio. She had a flower print dress on, and her hair was combed back.

"What do you think of the dress?" she asked Julian. "Édouard bought it for me and he paid quite a lot."

"Very nice," Julian said. "So, you like posing for Édouard?"

"Yes. Very much."

Julian looked at Victorine, wondering how long Édouard 's relationship with her would last, and what would happen to his marriage if Suzanne ever found out about it. Marriage requires commitment. That was the reason at thirty he had never married. He had never really been in love, although he had relationships with several women, but they went no further than the bedroom.

Chapter Fourteen

In 1863, a year after his father's death and a year after he met Victorine, Édouard exhibited three paintings at the Salon of the Refused. Louis-Napoleon created the Salon of the Refused as an alternative to the Salon which had rejected hundreds of paintings the year before.

The Salon of the Refused was a chance for Édouard to exhibit his paintings, but it was also a means for Louis Napoleon to dampen opposition to him for taking away many liberties, including freedom of the press and the right to a jury trial.

The Salon of the Refused opened on the afternoon of May 15 in a section of the Palais de l'Industrie in rooms adjoining the Salon. On the first day of the exhibit, the crowds were gigantic, with more than sixty thousand people attending.

Julian and Édouard stood outside the Palais de l'Industrie, waiting for the exhibit to open and for Nadar and Baudelaire to join them. The year before, Julian reminded Édouard, the Salon accepted one of his paintings, one more than so many other artists. It was a portrait of Édouard's father and mother.

"You should be proud," Julian said.

"I was never proud of him. He was a lower court judge who ruled on paternity suits and contested wills, nothing more," Édouard said. "He was a man with little ambition."

"It seems to me, he was a man dedicated to the institution he served," Julian said.

Stricken with paralysis a couple of years before his death, he was forced to resign his position on the court. During that time, he endured incredible pain that began with sores on his genitals, rectum, and mouth. The sores ulcerated creating serious complications.

"Yes, it was all about the institution and much less about ambition and self-esteem which are just as important. That's why my father was a man I didn't understand."

"Yes. But he didn't stop you from becoming a painter."

"No, he didn't, but he never accepted it."

"Fathers and sons are born to fight with each other. That's just how it is. I don't know why," Julian said, trying to make Édouard feel better about his relationship with his father.

Julian and Édouard waited an hour before the exhibit opened and Nadar and Baudelaire joined them. As they entered the hall, where Édouard 's "Luncheon on the Grass" was hanging, a crowd of about thirty people stood looking up at the painting and talking loudly.

At the center of the seven feet tall and eight and a half feet wide painting, a naked woman was seated on the grass having a picnic with two fully dressed men. A scantily dressed woman in the background was bathing herself.

"What do you think?" Édouard asked Nadar. "Isn't she striking?"

"I do like it," he said. "Yes. She is."

As they continued to view the painting, a tall, well-dressed man wearing a top hat walked up to it. He was carrying a long pole with a hook at the end and looked like he was getting ready to strike Édouard 's painting. But before he could, Nadar grabbed the man's arm and stopped him.

"What are you trying to do?" Nadar yelled at the man.

"I don't like it. It's ugly."

"That's too bad," Nadar said. He escorted the man out of the gallery and returned a few minutes later.

A group of gray-haired women pointed to the painting and laughed. One man standing next to the group of women shouted, "This is garbage," while a second man called the painting "disturbing, bizarre, and incomprehensible."

"Don't listen to them," Nadar said to Édouard.

"When I hear that I feel like giving up," Édouard said.

"But you won't."

Chapter Fifteen

Weeks after the Salon of the Refused opened, Charles Baudelaire came to Édouard 's studio.

Julian had gotten there earlier and was watching Édouard painting at his easel. When Charles arrived, the first thing Édouard asked him was why Jeanne wasn't with him. Édouard had painted her portrait the year before.

Jeanne was a voluptuous, tall woman with silky ebony skin and jet-black hair that flowed down her back, and Charles was madly in love with her. Despite his love, Jeanne treated Charles miserably. Together, they spent money wildly, she on clothes and jewelry, and he on paintings that often were worthless.

They were deeply in debt, so deep that to escape creditors, they moved from apartment to hotel to lodging house. Édouard often lent Charles money. He admired Charles and often told people he was France's finest poet, but also its unluckiest. The French government prosecuted Charles for a volume of poetry, *Flowers of Evil*. Some poems were judged indecent and several of them were banned from publication. Sometimes Charles acted crazy, but no matter how bizarre his behavior, Édouard always excused it.

"The last time I saw her was two weeks ago," Charles said, putting his arm on Édouard and taking him aside. "I need to borrow some money," he said, looking Édouard straight in the eye.

"What for, and how much?" Édouard asked.

"For last month's hotel bill, or they'll throw me out."

"How much? "Édouard asked again.

Despite them standing several feet from Julian, he could hear their conversation. "I can leave if you two want to talk," he said.

"No, Julian. Please stay," Édouard said. "I don't think Charles minds you being here and listening to us. Do you, Charles?"

"No. But I need fifty francs."

Julian sat back in his chair picked up a journal lying on an adjacent table and began to thumb through it.

"I'll lend you the money. I don't want to see you on the street. But you better not buy opium or anything else that will destroy your mind."

"You're a loyal friend."

"I want to paint a little longer and then we can go to lunch."

Édouard continued to paint while Julian sat reading the journal.

"I need to take care of something, but I'll be back," Baudelaire said.

"All right," Édouard said, wondering what Charles needed to do as he watched him walk out the door of the studio.

"Does he owe you a lot of money?" Julian asked.

Édouard put aside his brushes and palette. "Five hundred francs."

"What do you think has become of Jeanne?"

"I don't know, but she uses him."

"Do you know her well?"

"No. Not really. However, I learned a little more about her when she sat for me for the painting. She's a very interesting woman. She was twenty years old when she came from Haiti to Paris. Charles met her singing at one of those cabaret clubs on the

Champs Elysée."

"He saw her there?"

"Yes. You've read his poetry. You know how much of a romantic Charles can be."

Yes. I know."

"He gave her an enormous bunch of roses one day at the stage door and soon they were a couple."

"So why are you and Charles such good friends?"

"It's hard to give you a reason."

"You think alike?"

"No. Not Really."

"But you seem to be best friends."

"Yes. We've talked often about painting and art. I think my ideas have influenced how he thinks."

"I've heard some critics say to the contrary, that he's had a greater influence on your work than you've had on his ideas."

"No. The people who believe that haven't heard any of our conversations."

"I've always thought they were wrong."

"They are very wrong. We have argued over many other issues, but I think he accepts my views on art and I appreciate what he thinks."

"I would think, though, you have very different views on politics."

"Especially in politics. You know how strongly I feel about a republic, while Baudelaire would rather have an aristocracy. He believes in the power of aristocracy. For him, it is the primary form of legitimate government. I don't accept that. But because we are friends, we don't argue about it."

"It's a wonder a poet would have such political views. A poet, I would think, would have more democratic views."

"You are right, but as I said, Charles and I are friends."

Julian went back to reading his journal and Édouard continued to paint. When Charles returned, Édouard handed him several hundred francs. The three of them left the studio and got a carriage.

"Where will we have lunch?" Baudelaire asked.

"The Rotisserie Pavard."

"That's where we had lunch when we met," Baudelaire said.

"Five years ago," Édouard said. "Jeanne was with you."

"That's a long time ago."

While Charles and Édouard talked about their past together, Julian wondered what would become of Baudelaire and why some people were unlucky while others were not.

When they got back to the studio after lunch, Baudelaire quickly left. Julian looked at Édouard. "Why is Baudelaire so unlucky?" he asked.

"Sometimes you need to make your own luck. Charles hasn't learned that yet , but maybe someday he will," Édouard said.

Chapter Sixteen

Nadar convinced Édouard and Julian to join him for the maiden voyage of his twelve-story hot-air balloon, The Giant.

It was October 4, 1863, a day Julian would never forget. He took a carriage to the Champ de Mars, where the balloon was to be launched. The Giant was being inflated in the center of a huge grassy field. Standing around the balloon were a few hundred people.

Julian heard Édouard's voice as he walked toward the group of people. There was a young woman standing next to Édouard Julian didn't recognize.

"Ah, Julian. You made it," Édouard said with a smile.

"I wouldn't miss it for the world."

"Julian, I'd like you to meet Mademoiselle Trudeau. Marlene is Nadar's assistant."

"I'm delighted to meet you," Marlene said. Her voice was soft.

She had an innocent look about her and couldn't have been more than twenty. She smelled sweet, like lavender. Her hair was midnight black, and her eyes were as blue as the October sky.

"I'm very pleased to meet you," Julian said. He stumbled for something more to say to her. "What do you do for Nadar?" he asked, trying hard not to stutter.

"I help him take photographs."

Julian was pleased he didn't stutter and he wanted to keep the conversation going. "Working with Nadar must be exciting work.

"Yes. He's great to work for, and I look up to him."

"It seems there's a lot of work that goes into getting the balloon ready."

"Yes. Many hours to get it ready for the biggest event for the Champs de Mars since the first balloon lifted off from here some eighty years ago."

"I didn't know you knew so much about the history of balloon flight," Julian said.

"I don't. Marlene has been giving me a history lesson."

"So, you know so much about photography and balloon flight?" Julian asked.

"I know a little," Marlene said. She blushed and there was a twinkle in her eye as they all moved closer to the balloon.

"Tell me more about this giant balloon," Julian said.

"It's really an airborne wicker cottage under a 200-foot balloon."

"It's more like a flying chateau," Julian said, with a smile.

"There are several compartments and two cabins. There's also a lavatory and a storeroom."

"It looks like Nadar has spared no expense," Édouard said.

While his attention was on Marlene, Julian noticed the crowd around them getting larger and larger. It seemed all of Paris had come out.

"I bet he's done a very good job publicizing it. Nadar loves publicity," Julian said.

"You know him well," Marlene said.

"Yes. He's always impressed me."

"He also a very good businessman. He's charging the people standing around us one franc each to watch the balloon lift off," Marlene said.

"That won't make him rich," Julian said.

"He's also charging the nine passengers as much as he can," she said.

"Édouard and I are not paying anything."

"Of course. You're his friends and he values that friendship which doesn't have a price."

They were just a few feet from the balloon when Nadar stepped forward.

"Did you bring your papers, your passports?" Nadar asked.

"Yes, we did," Julian said.

"Good. We could wind up in Belgium."

"I hope you have food on board," Julian said.

"Do I go anywhere without food?" Nadar said.

"No. You don't," Julian said.

"What do you think of my ship?"

"It's a marvel," Julian said.

For a moment, Julian thought about how dangerous it could be. But as he looked at Marlene, he erased the thought from his mind. She was calm.

"What do you think of my assistant?" Nadar whispered to Julian after pulling him aside.

"She's very bright," Julian said

"Yes she is. She had good parents who instilled in her a thirst for knowledge. Her father was a doctor and her mother was a teacher. I knew them well. But they died in a fire about a year ago.

"I'm sorry to hear that."

"Her family meant so much to her. My wife and I have let her become a part of ours"

It was late in the afternoon before the balloon was filled. The spectators had become impatient, and some began chanting, *Let's go. Let's go.* Nadar and his wife, Ernestine, the two pilots, the nine paying passengers, and Édouard, Marlene, and Julian, took their turns climbing up the rope ladder and into the wicker gondola.

"Let go of everything," Nadar shouted to the men down on the ground. They unfastened the ropes that had kept the balloon in place, and it rose slowly.

"Quite a sight," Marlene said to Julian as they looked down on the crowd, getting smaller and smaller. The sound of the military band that had been playing for some time slowly faded away.

"We're climbing into that silent vastness," Nadar said.

"There you go again, being the philosopher," Julian said.

"If you say so," Nadar said.

Julian, Marlene, and Édouard sat next to each other, along with the nine paid passengers, on four wicker benches arranged around a massive table. Nadar and Ernestine sat at the head of the table.

"I hope they know what they're doing," Julian said, looking up at the two pilots outside on the deck above the gondola. They were talking to each other and seemed to be monitoring the balloon's movement as the wind slowly carried the party west.

The giant balloon had been in the air for more than two hours when Nadar announced it was time for dinner. He stood up and turned around to open the wicker cabinets behind him. The cabinet contained a heaping platter of ham. Another contained three platters with turkeys that were cooked to perfection and put aboard. Nadar reached for the platters and set them one by one on a table in front of him. He opened a third cabinet that stored several bottles of wine.

"This is very good wine," Nadar said as he opened each

bottle. Marlene got up and filled the passenger's glasses.

"Don't spill any. I paid a good price for the wine," Nadar said.

"Are you enjoying yourself?" Édouard asked Nadar.

"Of course, he is," Ernestine said.

Marlene sat back down next to Julian. He felt lightheaded from the wine and more relaxed. It was easier to talk to her.

"Have you ever thought of modeling?" Julian asked Marlene.

"No. Many of the women who model have a dark side."

"What do you mean?"

"You know what I mean, a dark side."

"Not all of them. Why do you ask?"

"Because I think you're an attractive woman and you'd make any painting come to life," Julian said.

"Come on," she said as her mouth curved into a smile.

"I mean it."

"I'd rather be smart. Being beautiful isn't as important."

"You would?"

"Yes."

There was something different about Marlene. If he had told another woman she was beautiful, she'd be thanking him.

They spent the next few hours talking until it was morning. As they watched the sun come up and then move across the sky, it got hotter and hotter. The balloon started to drift downward. It was losing altitude and everyone became silent. Suddenly, Julian heard Nadar shout orders at the pilots.

"We've got to get control of the balloon," Nadar yelled.

"Are you frightened?" Julian asked Marlene.

"No. I don't like being frightened."

But Julian saw Marlene's eyes widen. He looked around at

93

the other passengers and knew they were just as afraid as they were. It was a fear that made the heart beat quicker, tensed the muscles, and churned the stomach. Then he saw Marlene stand up and wave her arms over her head, trying to get everyone's attention.

"Please listen," she said. "The pilots know what they're doing. They'll get us down. Just be calm." Julian heard a struggling determination in her voice. When she finished trying to calm the passengers, she sat back down next to Julian. He reached for her hand and she grasped his. Julian watched one of the pilots venting the gas from the balloon so its descent could be more controlled. The wind had become stronger, helping to push the balloon down toward the ground. When the balloon finally touched the ground, it bounced around brushing against the trees. Julian watched as the balloon seemed headed for a locomotive. He was sure they would crash into it, but the train's engineer immediately stopped the train and the balloon just missed it. For several minutes, the balloon and its wicker gondola bumped along the ground before coming to a dead stop. Before coming to a stop, all of the passengers had been ejected from the gondola.

Marlene landed a few feet from Julian, and Édouard was several feet away. Julian yelled to Édouard, who shouted back that he was all right. The other passengers and the two pilots were less than twenty yards away. Within minutes, all of them were standing. Nadar and Ernestine walked toward them.

"Is everyone all right?" Nadar asked.

"I think so," Marlene said, holding Julian's hand.

Julian looked at Marlene. "I don't know if I'll ever go up again," he said.

"Yes, you will. I know you will," she said, wrapping her arms around him.

Chapter Seventeen

The day they got back to Paris, Julian invited Marlene to his apartment. All that day Julian wondered if she would come, but that evening, when he heard a knock on the door, he opened it and Marlene was standing there.

"You look surprised," Marlene said.

"No, I'm not. Aren't you going to come in?"

"Of course, I am."

"I know you told me you'd come but I wondered if you would.

"Why did you wonder?"

"I don't know why."

"You shouldn't have," Marlene said, as she walked to the couch in the center of the room and sat down. When Julian sat down next to her, he noticed a bruise on her arm.

"What's this?" he asked. "I thought you said you were all right and didn't get hurt."

"I didn't think I did until I noticed this bruise when I got up this morning."

"Does it hurt?" Julian asked

"It looks worse than it is."

"I 'll put a wet cloth on it and that will make the swelling down."

"You're very kind, but it's not necessary. Bumps and bruises don't bother me."

"Are you sure?"

"I said I'm fine."

Marlene glanced around the room. Julian had spent a few hours cleaning it up. He put away all the books scattered everywhere. He had a habit of reading just a chapter or two and then putting the book down and start reading another one. Sometimes he would go back to a book he had started and finish it, but that was rarely the case. Not finishing something was second nature and it went beyond books.

"Your place is immaculate."

"I must be honest. I'm not always that neat."

"I'm not either."

"That means we have something in common."

Julian got up from the couch and went over to a small cabinet in a corner of the room. He brought out a bottle of burgundy and two glasses. After he had filled them to the brim, he looked at Marlene. She had a questioning look on her face. Maybe, he shouldn't have filled them to the brim.

"I always fill the glass to the top," he said. "Does it bother you?"

"No. Not at all. But do you do it for every woman you invite to your apartment?" "No. Not every woman." He raised his eyes and smiled at her.

After several glasses of wine, and spending a couple of hours recapturing their balloon trip together, Julian felt relaxed. Marlene seemed to be at ease too. Julian had the same euphoric feeling he had the day before with her, only it was more intense. He had never felt this way for any other woman before. He moved closer to Marlene.

Julian looked directly at Marlene and blurted out, "Is it possible to fall in love with someone who you have just met?" He told himself he shouldn't have said that but it was too late to take his words back.

She answered immediately with no hesitation. "Maybe. Love is strange."

"Why do you say that?"

"That's what I think because sometimes people confuse love with lust."

"But sometimes they aren't confused and they know the difference and it's also possible that lust can turn into love."

"I suppose so," Marlene said. "But to me, love is finding out nothing in the world could make you feel any better. Don't you think?"

Julian didn't answer. Instead, he moved closer to Marlene and pressed his lips against hers. Several times she kissed him and then let her tongue dance in his mouth.

"It's getting warm in here," Julian said.

"Yes, it does seem very warm."

"What do you want to do?"

"If you asked me to stay the night, I would," Marlene said.

"Then, I'm asking you."

Taking Marlene's hand, Julian led her into his bedroom. He slowly undressed her. She raised her arms as he slipped off her dress and helped him take off her stockings and undergarments. When he saw her naked, he felt on fire. He ran his hands through her hair, as she unbuttoned his shirt and took it off. She smiled with eagerness as his trousers and then his underwear dropped to the floor.

They stood naked together looking at each other. Then he lifted Marlene up and carried her to his bed. Julian gazed at her breasts, her nipples seeking the pleasure of his mouth. She sighed softly as his tongue encircled each warm nipple. He planted soft kisses all over her body before moving to the warmth between her legs. She was wet and inviting and ready for him and helped him enter her slowly.

"I don't want us to forget this night, "she whispered, her body trembling in his arms.

"Nor do I," he said.

For five days, they spent every minute together. In the mornings, they walked in the Tuileries, and in the afternoons, Julian took her shopping at Le Bon Marche and other fancy stores. In the evenings, they dined at exclusive restaurants, coming home at night to their bed and enjoying each other's bodies.

On the fifth night, before they fell asleep, Julian looked into Marlene's eyes and asked, "Are you Happy?"

"Yes, I'm more than that."

Marlene fell asleep in Julian's arms. When Julian woke up the next morning and looked next to him for Marlene, he couldn't believe his eyes. She wasn't there. He jumped out of his bed and went looking for her. But she was gone. For a moment, he thought those five nights were a dream. How could he have been so lucky to find someone like Marlene? When he came back to the bedroom, he noticed a note lying on the top of his dresser. It took him just seconds to read it.

"I don't want to get involved, and that's what will happen if I stay another night. I'm sorry. Marlene."

Julian stared at the note. He couldn't believe she would break it off with just a note. How could she do that? He had been with other women, but this time there was meaning. He wanted to talk to her and rushed to get dressed. Then he flagged down a carriage and went directly to Nadar's workshop. When he got there, he found Nadar busy repairing the balloon's gondola.

"Do you know where Marlene is?" he asked.

"I'm sorry Julian, I don't. She came in early this morning, carrying a knapsack, filled with some of her clothes, and told me she was quitting," Nadar said.

"Did she say why?"

"No. She just said she was quitting and leaving Paris. Didn't she tell you?"

"No. All she left was a note that didn't make any sense. I don't understand it."

"I'm sorry, Julian. I don't either."

Chapter Eighteen

The next day Julian went to Édouard 's studio. On his way, all he could think about was Marlene. But he was determined not to say anything to Édouard about the note she left.

In his studio, Édouard stood at his easel, working on a painting of a nude woman reclining on a chaise lounge. There was a small black cat at her feet, and a black woman, who was holding a bouquet, stood behind her.

"I'll be able to finish it in another day or two," Édouard said.

"A lot of people, especially the men, are going to criticize it," Julian said. "They won't like that she's looking directly at them as if they were her clients."

"As long as the Salon accepts it. That's what matters to me."

Julian moved closer to the painting. "I know that's Victorine, but who is the black woman?"

"Her name is Laure. She reminds me a little of Clarissa who we met in Rio de Janeiro. Remember Clarissa?"

Julian took another look at the painting. "I do. Yes, she looks a little like Clarissa, although I remember her skin was much lighter. But that was a long time ago."

"It was a long time ago, but I never forget a woman I've known."

Édouard smiled and went back to the painting. Each brush stroke was loose, broad, quick and visible.

"That's what I like, the visible brush strokes that distinguish your paintings and, of course, the naked woman."

"What would Marlene say if she heard you talking that way?" Édouard asked.

"I don't know what she'd say."

"I get the impression you don't want to talk about Marlene."

"We should change the subject."

"If that's what you want."

"I've been meaning to ask you about your mother. How is she getting along since your father's death?"

"It's been very hard on her. She was very much in love with him."

"I thought it would be difficult for her. Did the doctors ever say what caused his illness?"

"No. They couldn't even tell us what they thought brought on his unusual behavior when he was still able to talk and be understood."

"What do you mean?"

"He became very religious and would lock himself in his room and pray for hours. He did that nearly every day. That's why my mother asked the archbishop to administer the last rites just before he died. But I would never want that."

"Why do you say that?"

"There was a time when I believed in religious rituals when I was young, and we'd all go to mass every Sunday. But now I don't know what to believe."

Chapter Nineteen

Julian was standing outside the Church de Saint-Germain-des-Pres waiting for Édouard, who was attending the funeral of Eugene Delacroix. When the service was over, Édouard came out of the church with two other men, Charles Baudelaire and Ernest Meissonier.

"I'm not one for these services, but it was striking," Édouard said to Julian who had walked over to meet him. "So many talked about how great an artist he was. I think I need to make some introductions."

Julian interrupted. "I remember the day you spent copying one of his paintings."

"I was about twenty years old when I copied his "The Barque of Dante." I think he must have been twenty-five when he painted it. But let me introduce everyone. Charles and Julian know each other. Julian Mercier is a journalist and has written for a number of Paris journals. Today at the funeral, I met Monsieur Ernest Meissonier and asked him to join us for dinner. He's one of this country's greatest painters."

"You paint history, don't you?" Julian said

"You could say that," Meissonier said. "Many of my paintings depict historic events. Five of them were shown at the 1861 Salon, while nine were exhibited at the 1855 Salon, and, the same number at the 1857 Salon."

"You've been more fortunate than most artists to have so many paintings accepted by the Salon," Julian said. He turned away from Meissonier to look at Charles, who was all skin and bones. "Monsieur Delacroix's death must have been hard on you."

"Yes, but it was also hard on Édouard and Monsieur Meissonier. We all considered Monsieur Delacroix a friend."

Julian looked again at Meissonier. "I would think you, Monsieur Meissonier, and Édouard would have a lot to talk about. If we walk to the café, you two can talk some more about painting, and Charles can tell me what's going on in Paris literature."

"Yes, I would like to hear more from Édouard on how he chooses the subjects, and why he chose to paint an absinthe drinker," Meissonier said.

"I'd love to learn from Monsieur Meissonier how he researches his subject, and sometimes spends months to be precise about the littlest detail," Édouard said, slowing down his jaunt for Charles to catch up.

After the two-mile walk to the Café Guerbois and before they could find a table, Édouard saw Pierre sitting alone and asked if they could join him.

As Meissonier was about to sit down, he looked directly at Pierre. "Don't I know you?" he asked Pierre. "Your face seems familiar."

"It's probably because of Édouard 's painting of *The Absinthe Drinker*. I was its subject." "You don't say."

"Monsieur Meissonier has served as a judge on several of the Salon juries," Édouard said.

"Édouard 's painting was rejected by the Salon. The only judge to vote in favor of it was Monsieur Delacroix," Pierre said.

"Yes, I know. We've just come from his funeral," Meissonier said.

103

"Tell me, Monsieur Meissonier, what does the Salon want for a painting to be accepted?"

"I can't speak for other judges. But I'll tell you what I find appealing, historical and classical subjects. What is also important is a highly finished style."

"Édouard 's paintings are much better than that."

"But many critics seem to like my approach."

"So you say," Pierre shouted at Meissonier.

Édouard jumped into the conversation. "We can argue about this another day."

Meissonier abruptly stood up and turned to leave the Café Guerbois. "I've got a long carriage ride ahead of me."

"You do have a long ride and we understand. It's been a pleasure talking with you," Edouard said, moving between Pierre and Meissonier. "I hope to see you again, soon."

"I look forward to that," Meissonier said.

After Meissonier had left the café, Pierre turned to Édouard. "What do you mean you hope to see him soon? He's arrogant, ugly, and mean. He shouldn't be judging your paintings."

Julian pulled Édouard aside and whispered, "I'm worried Pierre may do something to make sure Meissonier doesn't judge any more of your paintings."

"What do you mean?"

"I don't know exactly but it seems that he was so angry he might do something."

Chapter Twenty

Édouard Manet's Journal
October 28, 1863

Tomorrow, Suzanne and I will be married. I hope it's a better day than today, with all the rain. I want to see the sun.

I haven't picked up a brush to paint or a pencil to sketch for the last three weeks. Suzanne has found some time to play the piano, and I've done a lot of walking around the town.

I have thought a lot about Leon. At eleven, he looks more like his mother. He's growing up, and I'm sure he will someday be a fine man.

It is time for Suzanne and me to get married. I wonder what my life would be like if my mother had not brought Suzanne into our home. She came to teach Eugene and me to play the piano, and now she's going to be my wife. What if that had not happened? I sometimes think certain things in life are predestined.

It has been hard living a double life, presenting myself socially as the eligible son of a judge but secretly spending free time with my family. I kept up that duplicity for ten years until my father's death. But after his death last year, I don't have to continue the deception. I no longer have to hide my relationship with Suzanne. But people still wonder about my relationship with Leon.

When we return to Paris, we'll set up a home on the

Boulevard des Batignolles. We'll be a family. Let people think what they may.

I must admit it's hard to think of myself as a married man, but family is important to me. Sometimes there is lust in my heart. I think that lust is the bane of a man's existence. For me, it helps spark creativity. Victorine has helped spark that creativity. She's been my muse. I wonder if there will be any other woman like that.

It's strange to be thinking about Victorine tonight. I shouldn't have thoughts about her. But she knows how to please a man. There is a lot about Victorine that I admire. She wants to be a painter, and I admire that, although I know it's hard for a woman. She's lived a rough life.

I think about Victorine lying on the bed as I painted her before leaving for Holland. There were some warm moments. I can hear her saying, "You can do with me what you want."

Women, I love them all. It doesn't matter where they come from, whether they're rich or poor. It helps if they have attractive features. I do tire of this one or the other. I wonder if I'll tire of Suzanne. She is a good wife. When we first met, she excited me, especially with her music and watching her at the piano. I was seventeen then and today I am thirty-one. We began with a welcoming understanding of each other. We've been together for almost fourteen years, but she helps keep me focused on my art.

My friend Charles is right. Painting must find poetry in contemporary everyday places and capture modern life. There is no need to focus on dead civilizations when the world around is so alive.

Last night I dreamed Suzanne was standing alone in a field of wildflowers. All she was wearing was a white robe. I asked her to take off the robe, but she said she didn't want to. I looked up at the sky as a bolt of lightning struck the ground. Then I felt the wind against my face and smelled the scent of a woman. Suddenly, a young, slender woman with black hair and dark eyes appeared naked in the field. Suzanne walked away. Where are you going? I asked her. I'm going back to Holland, she said. I woke up sweating.

In the morning, the dream was fixed in my mind, like one of Nadar's photographs. Suzanne asked me if I had a bad dream during the night. I told her no and wondered what dreams were for, but I don't have an answer.

Chapter Twenty-One

Hundreds of painters descended on the Palais des Champs-Elysees the day before the 1864 Salon was scheduled to be open to the public. Julian and Édouard headed to the exhibition hall where the painters were putting the finishing touches on their works.

The pickle-like odor of turpentine and the scent of alcohol from the varnishes the painters were using to finish off their canvases permeated the hall.

"Can you smell that?" Édouard asked Julian, as they walked through the hall to where his two paintings, "The Dead Christ with Angels" and "Incident in the Bull Ring" would be on display.

"You don't have to be a painter to smell it," Julian said.

"I know. I asked because I was trying to break the silence. It's the silence that makes me more nervous."

"You're nervous because you worry too much about what people think."

When they reached where Édouard 's paintings hung, Julian stood looking intensely at "The Dead Christ with Angels." It was the first time Julian had seen the painting.

Julian stared at the massive canvas of the tortured cadaverous body of Christ. It was a massive painting, five by six feet. Christ's white torso was surrounded by two grieving and distraught winged angels, one with a golden-brown dress and the other with a burgundy gown. Streaks of color thickened on Jesus's face.

Reddish purple smudges on his forehead looked like dried blood. His nose and eye sockets were painted in dark hues and his mouth was half-open. An inscription on a rock was painted at the bottom of the canvas.

"What's the inscription?" Julian asked, moving closer to the painting to get a better look.

"It's from the Book of John, Chapter 20, verse 12."

"That's the verse that describes Christ's tomb being empty except for two angels."

"Yes, that's true. But I wanted to paint a dead Christ as a man."

"Where did that idea come from?"

"From a book I've been reading, *The Life of Christ* by Ernest Renan. He's the Hebrew scholar who has looked at the bible in historical and scientific terms rather than from a theological perspective."

"I haven't read the book but I'm aware of it. The Catholic Church has labeled Monsieur Renan a dangerous man."

"That's because he presents Jesus as entirely human, mortal and describes Mary Magdalene suffering from hallucinations in interpreting the Resurrection, that it was a fabrication based on the power of love."

"That belief would anger any Catholic."

"Renan argues Christ was a popular religious leader and a self-proclaimed Messiah who advocated the overthrow of Roman rule and the creation of a theocracy."

"Do you believe that?"

"It's something to think about, but it's not important what I believe."

"What does your friend Pastor Abbe Hurel think of your painting?"

"He hasn't seen it yet. But I told him I was going to paint a dead Christ with angels and it would be a variation of Mary at the sepulcher."

"When he sees it, you may not be friends anymore."

"He's a very tolerant priest."

"The critics are not going to be as tolerant."

"Some may be tolerant, and some may not be," Édouard said looking across the room at several artists crowded in front of two paintings. When Édouard and Julian went to see what had captured their attention, they saw two of Meissonier's paintings.

One of them was small, The Battle of Solferino", a painting about twenty by thirty inches, depicting Louis-Napoleon on his horse in a battle scene. The other one was much larger. "The Campaign of France" was about a foot and a half by two and a half foot, showing Napoleon leading his soldiers into defeat.

They stared at the paintings for several minutes until they heard one of the artists say Meissonier had come into the room. Julian turned around to see Meissonier stop for a moment to look at Édouard's "The Dead Christ with Angels" and then walk toward them.

"I don't see your friend Pierre with you today," Meissonier said.

"No, he's not," Édouard said. "Why did you ask?"

"That's too bad. I got the feeling when I met him, he didn't like me. But I would have been pleased to show him my two paintings anyway," Meissonier said.

"Yes. I'm sure Pierre would have liked your painting of Louis-Napoleon," Julian said. "But did it take you four years to complete? That's a long time."

"If something is worth doing, it's worth doing well."

"What did you think of my "The Dead Christ with Angels?"

110

Édouard asked Meissonier.

"I'd rather not say."

"You must have some thoughts about it."

"If you must know what I think, I'll tell you. It's blasphemy."

"Édouard, I think we need to get going," Julian said, grabbing Édouard and pushing him toward the door.

"Why did you do that?" Édouard asked Julian as they rushed through the hall and onto the street.

"I didn't want you to get into a fight with Meissonier for two reasons. One, he could be part of a Salon jury to judge one of your paintings. You are lucky he apparently was not a judge for this Salon. And two, if Pierre heard you got into a fight with Meissonier, I don't know what would happen. I think it's possible Pierre would want to kill Meissonier."

Chapter Twenty-Two

One day in June 1865, Édouard, Julian, and Pierre jumped into a carriage outside Edouard's studio on their way to the Hippodrome de Longchamp, which was located on the western edge of the city between the banks of the Seine and the Bois de Boulogne, a vast public park. People began to arrive at the racetrack early in the morning.

Huge crowds of all ranks and classes had come for the races and to watch Gladiateur, the French thoroughbred favored to win the Grand Prix de Paris. They were the well-heeled and the working class. They shared Longchamp but were segregated from each other. The well-heeled sat in the grandstands on upholstered chairs while the working class watched from the bleachers on wooden benches or sat on the grass.

Several buildings bordered the racetrack. The most elaborate of the buildings was the Emperor's Pavilion, a five-story structure with an open-air observation deck. Louis-Napoleon, accompanied by his wife Empress Eugenie, sailed down the Seine and when they arrived at Longchamp, they strolled by the crowds on their way to the observation deck.

"The sight of that dictator is sickening," Édouard mumbled. "But I wouldn't give up my seat in the grandstands to avoid the view."

"Why are we sitting in the grandstands?" Julian asked. "We belong in the bleachers."

"You're wrong. We belong in the grandstands," Pierre said.

"Édouard, me and you."

"What do you mean?" Julian asked.

"I mean you, too. People look at you and what do they see? Edouard's shadow," Pierre said. "That means you should be sitting in the grandstands."

"I strongly disagree with you."

"Neither of you knows what you're talking about," Édouard said, as he took out his sketch pad and started drawing the people sitting in the grandstands. "I can't be moved."

He watched several women in perfectly tailored dresses and beautifully coiffed hair marvel at their lace parasols. They had walked arm in arm with their men in top hats and waist coats who escorted them to their seats in the grandstand.

Édouard kept busy sketching and managed to miss the first five races. But he put his sketch pad away and joined Julian and Pierre when Gladiateur came to the starting line.

"Who are you going to bet on?" Julian asked Pierre.

"On Gladiateur to win," Pierre said, with certainty in his voice.

"You haven't been lucky all day with your bets," Julian said. "None of your picks have won or placed or even showed in the five races you bet on."

"Gladiateur is a safe bet. Maybe Pierre will be lucky this time," Édouard said.

The horses began to line up at the starting line, but Gladiateur who was in place moved back from it.

"What's the matter with Gladiateur?" Pierre asked Julian.

"I have no idea," Julian said. As his words left his lips, Gladiateur managed to settle down and was chasing the other horses who were several lengths ahead of him.

"I think he's picking up speed," Pierre said with some hope

113

in his voice.

When the horses rounded the last turn, Gladiateur had moved from fourth to second. Turning into the stretch, Gladiateur unleashed a furious kick, charging on the outside and easily winning the race by a length.

"What a horse," Julian shouted, patting Pierre on the back, as Louis-Napoleon walked onto the field. "This is a great day for France and a great day for Gladiateur. We should all be very proud," Louis-Napoleon said as the crowd cheered.

"What does that fool know about horses?" Pierre mumbled.

"Watch out. You don't want someone to hear you," Julian said.

"I won't say anything more," Pierre said.

"You're a very lucky man," Julian said. "You started out the day losing and now it's turned around for you."

Chapter Twenty-Three

It was August 1865, when Édouard and Julian traveled to Madrid. One of the reasons for the trip was so Édouard could clear his mind of all the ridicule he had experienced at the Salon. But the major reason for his trip to Madrid was to visit the Prado and view Diego Velasquez's paintings.

Édouard and Julian were staying at a new hotel that had just opened. Hungry after arriving, they went to the hotel dining room for lunch. It was empty except for one gentleman sitting alone at a table a few feet away.

Every few minutes, Édouard ordered a different dish and tasted it. Then he would angrily reject the dish saying it was so bad he couldn't eat it. Each time he sent the waiter away, the man sitting alone called the waiter back. He ate each dish Édouard had sent back. Julian heard the man tell the waiter many times how much he liked the food. Édouard, who had been keenly observing the man, suddenly got up and marched over to him.

"Sir. Are you doing this simply to insult me?" Édouard said. "Are you trying to make a fool out of me?"

"No, nothing of the kind."

"So, you are not doing it because you know who I am and you are trying to insult me?"

Julian was silent as he looked on listening to their conversation.

"No sir, I don't know who you are. Why should I? For the last few weeks, I've been in Portugal and I nearly died of hunger there. To me, this hotel's cuisine is exceptional, and I wouldn't send any of it back."

"You say you've just come from Portugal. I'm from Paris which no one would argue has the best restaurants and the finest food anywhere."

"I understand you, sir. I'm also from Paris. Maybe you've heard of me. You seem like someone who may have heard of me because I am so well-known. My name is Theodore Duret and I'm a journalist What's your name sir?"

"Yes. I think I've heard of you. Aren't you the art critic? You should know my name. It's Édouard Manet. As you may be aware, I've been dragged through the mud many times."

"Ah yes. Manet, the painter."

"Yes, the painter, who is often laughed at just by walking along the boulevard."

"Yes, I'm an art critic. But I would disagree with those who make fun of you and your paintings. I've seen some of them and they should be praised."

"You see Édouard. Not everyone mocks you or your paintings," Julian said. "Maybe, Monsieur Duret would like to join us tomorrow when we go to the Prado."

"Yes. I would like to join you. I had planned on going to the Prado tomorrow. It would be a pleasure to hear what Monsieur Manet has to say about Diego Velasquez's work."

The next morning, Julian, Édouard, and Duret arrived at the Prado and hurried to gaze at Velasquez's Las Meninas.

Édouard stood silent , his eyes on the painting of the main chamber of the Royal Alcazar, with several figures from the Spanish court.

"He has captured a moment in time," Édouard said. painting.

"You see just behind the entourage; Velazquez is working on a

116

portrait of himself on a large canvas and he is looking outward."

"Yes, he is wearing an insignia of the Order of Santiago, which I had heard about," Duret said. "They say the king awarded the honor to Velazquez."

"That's the recognition a great painter deserves," Julian said.

"That's not how many of them are recognized in France," Duret said looking at Édouard.

"No, it certainly is not."

"Look at the brushwork and the interplay of light and shade," Julian said.

"I wonder what Velasquez's paintings would be like if he had the paint tubes in his day that artists use today," Duret said, looking more closely at the painting.

"Working with oil paint in the open air has not been easy," Manet said. "But the paint tubes we have had for the last twenty years have made the difference."

They continued to go back to the Prado for several days until Julian and Édouard decided it was time to go back to Paris. Duret joined them for the trip back.

At the border between France and Spain, in the French town of Hendaye, they were asked for their passports. Édouard handed his to an official. The official stared at Édouard with astonishment.

"So, you're the painter of those monstrosities," he said. The other people crossing the border, who stood behind them, stared. Julian worried whether Édouard's anger would get the better of him.

"I wouldn't call them monstrosities," Édouard said politely. "They're works of art."

"Yes. That's what they are," Duret said.

Chapter Twenty-Four

One day in May 1867, Julian stood next to Édouard, looking at one of his paintings at the opening of his one-man show. He told Julian he was concerned his paintings weren't getting the recognition they deserved so he had the wooden pavilion where they stood built to exhibit Édouard 's paintings.

Édouard had wanted to show his paintings at the International Exposition and the Salon that year, but they were rejected. He built the pavilion across from the site of the Exposition, expecting the critics and the public who came to see the Exposition would also visit his exhibit which included fifty of his paintings.

The International Exposition was Louis Napoleon's answer to the London International Exhibition of 1862. It was expected to draw people from Paris and from around the world. They would come and also experience the dramatic transformation of Paris. The city had undergone a major transformation from being a medieval overcrowded city to a modern one. Louis Napoleon appointed Baron Haussmann to transform the city by demolishing the slums and building fashionable apartment houses. The streets were broadened and beneath them, new lines for lighting and a new water and sewer system were constructed.

"I find it quite extraordinary that Louis Napoleon's exhibition will be the reason the public comes to see your paintings," Julian said.

"Yes, it is ironic in view of what I think about the monarchy."

As Julian and Édouard stood in front of his painting of "The Absinthe Drinker," they watched Nadar walk into the pavilion. When he saw Édouard and Julian, he rushed to greet them.

"This will be as good as the International Exposition for showing your paintings," Nadar said.

"I hope it will be," Édouard said.

The one-man show was not the only thing on Édouard 's mind. For the last several nights he hadn't been able to sleep; he was worried about the health of his friend Baudelaire who was suffering from aphasia and couldn't speak.

"How is Charles doing?" Édouard asked Nadar, who had just gone to see Baudelaire at the clinic where he was being treated.

"I'm sorry to say, I don't think he's doing very well. He still can't talk. The only two words that come out of his mouth are 'holy Christ.'"

"Every time Susanne and I have visited him, he's looked terrible," Édouard said. "He sits in that big armchair, hands white, his eyelids swollen and his eyes vacant. There is no trace of emotion on his face."

"He's at the clinic that specializes in hydrotherapy," Julian said, joining in on the conversation. "Isn't there anything they can do for him? It must be terrible for a poet who now is unable to speak a word."

"Nothing seems to work," Nadar said. "He has a pleasant room on the ground floor and I noticed two of Édouard 's paintings hanging on one of the walls."

"I know. When I saw the paintings, I felt honored," Édouard said." He's someone who understands my work. And I understand him."

"His mother was there when I saw him. She brought him back from Brussels, hoping he could get better care in Paris,"

Nadar said.

"Yes, I know he wanted to come back to Paris. He used to love walking in the city, although he has been mourning the loss of its medieval charm," Édouard said. "I knew he really wanted to come back when I wrote to him in Brussels. I told him I wished he was here and complained to him about the insults I've had to endure from some critics over my paintings."

"I'm sure he had something to say to you about that," Nadar said.

"Charles wrote he had to do his best to show me my value. Then he asked me if I thought I was the first man placed in such a situation. Is your talent greater than someone like Wagner? he wrote. Then he reminded me that the great composer was often ridiculed and it didn't kill him."

"That's what he would say," Nadar said.

"He showed me how much of a friend he has always been. I hate to see him suffering. He's forty-six, just ten years older than me, and I can't stand what he's going through."

"Maybe I should see him," Julian said. "He must feel terrible not being able to speak. I sometimes stutter but I couldn't imagine if I couldn't speak."

Julian went to see Baudelaire two weeks later. Four months after the opening of Édouard 's one-man show, Charles died.

Édouard and Julian attended the funeral. When Edouard spoke to the few mourners present about Baudelaire, Julian wondered if he was also thinking about Charles' thwarted career as a poet and his pursuit to be a great painter.

Chapter Twenty-Five

At the same time as the opening of his one-man show, Édouard began work on a new painting. He was at his studio when Nadar arrived and came in with a newspaper folded, under his arm

"Have you read this?" Nadar bellowed, taking out his newspaper and pointing to an article.

"No, I've been working all morning," Édouard said. "I wanted to get some work done before Julian and I went to the pavilion."

"You should read the newspaper before you paint in the morning," Nadar said loudly. "They executed Maximilian in Mexico."

"I read the newspapers," Édouard said. "They captured him, but I didn't know about his execution."

"It's shocking," Julian said, getting up from sitting in the chair in the corner of the studio. "It's another one of Louis-Napoleon's big mistakes, getting Maximilian to agree to become Emperor of Mexico. That shouldn't have happened. It wouldn't have happened if France hadn't gone into Mexico."

In 1861, Mexico defaulted on its debt and Louis-Napoleon saw it as an opportunity to carve out a dependent empire from the Mexican territory. Allied troops from France, Spain, and Britain invaded Mexico to recoup debts owed to them by the Mexican government. French occupancy of the country followed.

Napoleon offered to make Austrian Archduke Ferdinand Maximilian emperor of Mexico. The next year Maximilian was installed emperor. France's control of the country weakened and in 1866 Napoleon withdrew the French troops. When Louis-Napoleon ended his occupation of Mexico, Maximilian stayed. He was captured by Mexican forces on May 16, 1867, convicted, and sentenced to death. On June 19, 1867, a firing squad executed him.

"Louis-Napoleon also made another great mistake," Nadar said.

"Yes, not getting Maximilian out. He didn't deserve this," Julian said." I'm so angry. It's Louis-Napoleon who should have been shot. What's happening to France?"

"I don't know what's happening, but this was wrong, and I must do something about it. I'm going to paint a painting that will make Louis-Napoleon tremble," Édouard said.

Édouard looked straight at Nadar. "There must be photographs of the execution I can use to begin my painting," Édouard said.

"I'll help you if I can," Julian said. "I would love to see Louis-Napoleon shamed. He's gotten away with too much for too long."

"I'm uncertain any photographs exist," Nadar said. "But it would be my guess that some do, and they'll show up. I'll try to find one. My blood is boiling about this."

The notice of Maximilian's execution appeared in *Le Figaro* on July 8. On August 11, *Le Figaro* published a smuggled report on the execution. Related photographs were soon reproduced and available. Before the end of August, Nadar could buy a photograph of the execution and gave it to Édouard, who began work on the painting .

Édouard hastily went to work on the painting, making a series of sketches. As a basis for the painting, he used photographs of Maximilian and his generals, Miguel Miramon and Tomas Mejia. After that, he got a photograph of the firing squad killing Maximilian and the generals that Nadar acquired from a dealer later jailed for distributing prints. In one of the three paintings Édouard completed between 1867 and 1869, he made sure that one of the soldiers had a goatee beard similar to Louis-Napoleon's.

Chapter Twenty-Six

"She's beautiful," Édouard said under his breath to Julian. "She" was Berthe Morisot, who was with her sister Edma, copying a Rubens at the Louvre. It was a year after Édouard painted "The Execution of Maximilian," one late July morning in 1868. Henri Fantin-Latour, who had painted Édouard 's portrait introduced Édouard and Julian to two women. Édouard was thirty-six and Berthe was twenty-seven.

"So, you are Édouard Manet," Berthe said in a soft voice. "You have quite a reputation, Édouard Manet."

Édouard looked at her for a minute before he spoke. She was elegant, aloof, and slender, with pearl black hair and emerald-green eyes. "Why do you say that?"

"You know why, Édouard," Julian said.

"So, you probably heard that guards were needed to protect my painting "Olympia" from vandals at the Salon."

"Yes, and the Salon officials protected your painting by moving it to a less conspicuous place, to the same room my painting, 'Etude,' was hanging," Berthe said.

"Such abuses I have to withstand, Mademoiselle. It is Mademoiselle?"

"Yes. It is mademoiselle," she said.

"Enough of that banter," Henri interrupted. "We have ignored Julian and Edma."

"Yes, and that is not polite," Berthe said.

"I am very pleased to meet you, Monsieur Manet," Edma

said with a smile.

"You are much more polite than your sister," Édouard said.

"What is your last name, Julian?"

"It's Mercier, Mademoiselle."

"And what do you do, Monsieur Mercier?" Edma asked.

"I'm a writer. I write for *Le Figaro.* Someday, I would like to be an art critic," Julian said, realizing he did not stutter the words. He felt comfortable with the two ladies and Henri.

"It's been boiling," Henri said. "I don't enjoy hot weather."

"I don't like the hot weather either, but it's a lot better than the cold we had to deal with in January," Edma said.

"The snowstorm just after New Year's was awful," Berthe said. "I feel for the poor people who suffer from the cold a lot more than we do."

"You are right, Mademoiselle Morisot," Édouard said. "We have nothing to complain about."

"I enjoy the first snowfall. It's so beautiful," Berthe said.

"Yes. I enjoy walking the streets of Paris after the first snowfall," Édouard said.

"What else do you like, Monsieur Manet?" Berthe asked.

"What do you mean?"

"Do you enjoy horses? Do you like dogs? What makes you happy?"

"I enjoy the time I spend painting more than anything else."

"Yes. I feel the same way," Berthe said.

"And I like dogs," Édouard said. "I have a Prince Charles Spaniel, which I named Louis."

"After the Emperor?" Berthe asked.

"Yes. But of course."

"You and Édouard are monopolizing the conversation," Henri said.

"We don't want to do that," Édouard said. "What do you enjoy, Mademoiselle?" Édouard said, looking directly at Edma.

"I enjoy painting, but there are so many other things I like to do. I like to read novels," Edma said.

"You don't have to ask me," Julian said with a grin. "You know what I like? Horse racing."

"I know," Édouard said. "Julian and I love going to the Longchamp Hippodrome at the Bois de Boulogne.

"We saw Gladiateur win the Grand Prix de Paris in 1865. He was quite a horse. As you probably know, he won the English Triple Crown earlier that year. Do you know anything about horse racing, Mademoiselle Morisot?" Édouard said, looking at Berthe.

"No, I'm sorry I don't. I don't think I have ever been to Longchamp to watch the horses race. We do spend a lot of time on the Normandy coast. I enjoy the beaches there and the wonderful cliffs," Berthe said. "But maybe a horse race would be exciting."

"I love the coast," Julian said. "I've been to Boulogne, which is exquisite."

"Yes, it is beautiful," Henri said. "My apologies, but I must leave you. I have an appointment for a portrait I'm doing. Julian, would you and Édouard be so kind as to escort Edma and Berthe home safely?"

"Of course," Édouard said as he grabbed Berthe's arm and pulled her aside.

"I think you would be an excellent subject for one of my paintings?" Julian heard Édouard whisper to Berthe. "Is that something you would like?"

"Yes. Maybe I would, she said." As you can see, I'm just as polite as my sister."

"I can see that."

Chapter Twenty-Seven

That day in July when Édouard met Berthe and her sister, Edma, at the Louvre, he invited her to attend one of his mother's soirees. His mother was at her best presiding over these elegant affairs, which were held weekly and attended by writers, critics, musicians, intellectuals, and painters. The men sported full dinner dress with black tie while the women wore silk dresses, with their hair in elaborate coiffures. Maids circulated the room, offering drinks and food.

Berthe attended a soiree in September. Édouard had looked forward to it for two months. It was unusually warm; it felt more like a day in July than in September.

Julian watched Madame Manet stroll around the large main room talking with the guests, making certain they were enjoying themselves, while Édouard greeted the people at the door. At least a couple of dozen guests were already there, some standing and others sitting at small round tables.

Suzanne was seated at the piano in another room next to the main parlor, playing Chopin, her favorite composer.

"You can't play Chopin all evening. You know others," Madame Manet whispered to Suzanne.

Édouard greeted Berthe and a guest she brought at the door and then escorted them into the main room. Berthe was dressed in a flowing white gown, accentuating her jet-black hair. Julian could see from where he was standing, she was wearing a black ribbon around her neck with a locket that encased three violet flowers.

Julian looked to see who Berthe had brought with her. Édouard, Berthe, and the woman with her made their way over to Julian.

"This is my very good friend, Elizabeth Gardner," Berthe said to Julian.

"Mademoiselle Gardner, what a pleasure," Julian said, giving her a kiss on each cheek. "My guess is that you're a painter like Mademoiselle Morisot?"

"Yes, I am. Painting is something that keeps me busy." Mademoiselle Gardner said with a smile.

"You're too modest, Elizabeth. She's the first American woman to exhibit at the Salon."

"Perhaps I am."

"What made you want to become a painter? " Julian asked.

"To some extent it was the challenge it posed for me as a woman."

"That's so true. It's the same challenge many women like you and Mademoiselle Morisot face."

"But many of us find ways to be successful."

"Tell me what brought you to Paris?" Julian asked.

"I came here with another woman to study. She's been a student of Thomas Couture."

As soon as Édouard heard Thomas Couture's name, he interrupted. "I was a student of his for nearly six years. But we didn't see eye to eye."

"What do you mean?" Mademoiselle Gardner asked.

"He placed too much emphasis on classical compositions."

"There is something to be said for the classical approach."

"With all due respect, I couldn't disagree with you more."

"It all comes down to being able to compromise. I wouldn't

have been able to get into the drawing school in the Gobelin Tapestry Factory if I hadn't compromised my principles. Women were not accepted there. To get into the school I had to dress up as a boy. I didn't want to do that, but I had to."

"I can imagine that must have been very hard,"

"It was. Every day I had to travel to the school as a boy."

"You did that every day?"

"Yes, and I had to apply to the police for a permit that would allow me to wear men's clothing."

"That doesn't seem right to me," Julian interjected. "If a woman wants to study to be a painter, she should be allowed to go to the same school that a man can attend, and she shouldn't have to dress up like a boy."

"You're absolutely right Julian," Berthe said. "No woman should have to do that. Don't you think so, Édouard?"

"I agree Julian's right."

"Is that all you have to say about it?"

"What else should I say?" Édouard said. "I know what it's like to fight for something."

Julian again interjected. "Édouard 's told me many times how much he admires your work, Berthe, and if a woman wants to be a painter no one should be able to stop her."

"That's exactly what I have said many times," Édouard said, turning to Berthe and whispering, "I should have told you how exquisite you look tonight."

Édouard's brother, Eugene, who was standing several feet away, talking to a group of men, came over to where Édouard was standing and put his hand on his shoulder.

"I'm sorry. Let me introduce myself. I'm Eugene Manet, Édouard's brother."

"Good evening, Eugene," Berthe said. "I'd like you to meet

my friend, Elizabeth Gardner. She's a painter."

"Are you a painter like your brother Édouard?" Elizabeth asked.

"No, he's much better than I could ever be, although he would like me to get serious about it."

The noise of people talking faded away as Suzanne began to play a waltz. Several couples walked to the center of the room to dance.

"Would you like to dance?" Édouard said to Berthe.

"I don't know if I should."

"Why not?"

"I don't know why not. Yes, that would be nice.'

Édouard walked Berthe to the center of the room. He placed his right hand around her waist, behind her back. As she placed her left hand on Édouard's shoulder and they joined hands, Julian watched the two begin slowly to whirl around the floor. Berthe looked up at Édouard and rested her head on his chest.

When the waltz was over, Suzanne went back to playing Chopin, Berthe and Édouard walked over to Eugene and Elizabeth.

"If you'll excuse us for a minute," Eugene said. He motioned to Édouard and took him aside. "Suzanne doesn't mind you dancing with another woman?"

"This is Berthe's first visit to our home. I wanted to make sure she enjoyed herself. So, I asked her to dance. Suzanne wouldn't mind."

Julian who had sat out the dance caught up with Édouard and Eugene. They started to walk back to Berthe and Elizabeth, but then Édouard noticed a young woman he knew sitting by herself. He waved at her and they walked over to where she was sitting.

"Eugene, Julian, this is Eva Gonzales. Eva's a student of

mine. She also wants to be a painter. Julian is a good friend of mine and Eugene's my brother. I keep trying to persuade him to become a painter."

"I hope you're enjoying yourself," Eugene said.

"Yes, I am," Eva said.

"It's good to see you, Eva," Édouard said. "But we've got to get back to some friends of Eugene."

"Yes. That's fine. Thank you for introducing me to your friend and your brother."

As the three walked back to where Berthe and Elizabeth were standing, Édouard told Eugene and Julian about Eva. She wanted to attend the Ecole des Beaux-Arts, but it wouldn't accept women who wanted to study art. She has had other teachers, but she also wanted to study with him. In return, she agreed to model and let him paint her portrait.

When they reached Berthe and Elizabeth, Berthe asked who was the young woman she saw them with.

"I'm painting her portrait," Édouard said. "She's a very good model."

"She is. That's good, "Berthe said. pausing for a moment. "It's getting late. It's probably time for us to leave."

Édouard and Eugene walked Berthe and Elizabeth out the front door.

"Isn't she heavy?" Berthe mumbled to Elizabeth.

"Who are you talking about?" Elizabeth asked.

"The young woman who is having her portrait painted by Édouard," Berthe whispered.

"No. I don't think she's heavy. I think she's quite attractive."

Julian, who was standing at the door, was able to hear what Berthe said. But he turned his attention to a man selling sugared water outside, a few feet away. The man almost knocked the four of them down as they were leaving. He was one of about a dozen men selling the water, making it difficult for those trying to get a carriage. Julian walked toward Édouard to see if he could help.

"They could have knocked Berthe and Elizabeth down," Édouard said.

"It's almost impossible to get by them with their tin cans strapped to their back and all those cups hanging from hooks swaying as they go down the street, "Julian said.

Despite the sugared water sellers, Elizabeth and Berthe were able to get a carriage within a few minutes.

"It's a wonder more people didn't get hurt," Édouard said.

"I know," Julian said. "We were lucky. That's the old Paris going away."

Chapter Twenty-Eight

Édouard Manet's Journal
August 12, 1868

I wonder what makes a man lose interest in one woman and become attracted to another? I know physical attraction is essential, but it's more complex than that.

I asked Berthe to model for me because I wanted to spend more time with her. She is more attractive than Victorine and more interesting. I know my responsibilities, Suzanne and Leon. Family is important, but sometimes I forget.

Berthe seems so confident. I'm almost stirred as much by her confidence as I am by her beauty. She's been modeling for me every day for a week, coming in for a few hours each afternoon. Yesterday evening, Berthe and I had dinner together. While holding Berthe's hand in the dimly lit restaurant, she looked into my eyes, and I looked into hers. She said my paintings make her think of a wild, not-quite-ripe fruit. Then she asked why painting was so important to me. I told her it gives me meaning and then I asked why it was so important to her. For the same reason it is to you, she said.

Berthe has seen the portrait of Suzanne in my studio. I wonder what she thinks about it. She knows I was immediately attracted to her when we met in the Louvre. She acts as if she is interested in me. I would like to take her to bed. She talks about the passion she has for painting. It's the only way she has found to liberate her passion. Would she feel that passion for me?

We left the restaurant and took the same carriage. The driver had his eyes on the road and could not see my hand as I slowly reached up to caress Berthe's smiling face. She closed her eyes. Do you want me to kiss you? I asked, and she said yes. Then I kissed her on the mouth, and she kissed me. back. I could feel the passion in her kiss.

Chapter Twenty-Nine

In July 1870, the same year Édouard was lucky enough not to get killed in a duel with Duranty, France was at war with Prussia. France had declared war with Prussia, but the French army was ill- prepared. The Prussians quickly defeated the French army, and on September 2 Louis-Napoleon along with eighty thousand men, surrendered to Prussian Chancellor Otto Von Bismarck.

Louis-Napoleon's administration was overthrown by a popular uprising in Paris. The uprising forced the creation of a new government. The Prussians immediately advanced to Paris. By September 19, the Prussians had surrounded Paris, and a horrible siege began.

Édouard was thankful he had put Suzanne, Leon, and his mother on a train to Oloron-Sainte- Marie in the Pyrenees, 400 miles away from Paris.

Édouard and Julian volunteered for the National Guard. Their primary job was to defend Paris, taking positions behind the barricades that were built up around the city.

Édouard had moved his paintings to the cellar of Theodore Duret. More than a dozen paintings, including "Olympia" and "Luncheon on the Grass," were moved to the cellar. "If I should get killed," Édouard told Duret, "You can take your choice of "Olympia" or "Luncheon on the Grass."

"I hope they'll be safe. The Prussians would probably burn them," Édouard said to Julian with a worried look.

It was October 25. The two men were tired. They couldn't

sleep because of the shelling. They had watched a magnificent aurora borealis and a brilliant white one flickering in the sky.

In the morning, Julian and Édouard walked to the Place de la Concorde to line up with the National Guards for a review. The Guards lined the boulevards from the Place de la Concorde to the Madeline and to the Place de la Concorde. In the air was the sound of dozens of people who watched the review, singing the "La Marseillaise."

"I wonder if the Prussians are regretting their decision to take Paris," Édouard said.

"They must have thought it would be much easier," Julian said.

Julian watched a crowd of a dozen people surround a hunched-over man. He was selling caricatures of Louis-Napoleon looking like a pig.

"He is a pig," Édouard said as he reached into his pocket for a franc and handed it to the man.

The siege continued into November. Some 400 shells fell on the city each evening. The Prussians fired their guns late into the night making it nearly impossible to sleep. The shells struck everywhere; chapels were hit, as well as schools and factories.

People were hoping for a major offensive to break the siege, counting on the provinces. But the siege continued to make life worse. Smallpox broke out in the city. Children were dying of scurvy. Mules and horses were being eaten. Butcher shops were selling dogs, cats, and rats.

Many living in Paris left before the siege. But there were those who stayed. Berthe stayed, as did her friend, Elizabeth Gardner. Mademoiselle Gardner and her friend, Imogene Robinson, who had a studio near Luxembourg Gardens continued to paint during the siege.

Édouard and Julian went with Berthe to visit Elizabeth a few times. They talked about the war and always about painting. During one of those visits, Édouard brought up the subject of the Salon.

"I know this war is on all our minds, but I sometimes try to think of other things. I wonder whether we will again be able to exhibit at the Salon."

"It's important to me, as I know it is to you. I, like you, have worked very hard to have my paintings accepted by the Salon," Elizabeth said. "I hope I will have that opportunity again."

"You have an independent spirit, Mademoiselle Gardner," Édouard said, smiling for a moment.

"You do too, Monsieur Manet."

"You should come more often to my mother's soirees when life gets back to normal."

"I would like that."

Berthe gazed at Édouard with a concerned look. "But the Salon is not the only place," Berthe said. "What's important is that people get to see your paintings. Sometimes it's the Salon, but sometimes it's not."

Chapter Thirty

Édouard Manet's Journal
September 1870

Sometimes, Berthe seems jealous of other women. I wonder if she's jealous of Eva, but she shouldn't be. She's not jealous of Suzanne. Maybe that's because the other women are young and attractive, and Suzanne has lost the glow she once had

Berthe's friend Elizabeth is feisty. I'm fascinated by her when she switches from English to French, Italian, and German. It makes the people she's talking to feel at ease. But Berthe shouldn't be jealous. Although, I would be jealous of her if she acted like me with other men.

Lovers are never rational.

I've told her that sometimes I wish I could give up my family and be with her all the time. But we both know that's impossible. Yet, I worry she will give up on me for someone else. She worries about getting old and not having a husband. She wants children.

The only good thing about the siege is that we've been able to slip away when I'm off duty to be with each other for an hour or two. I can't stop thinking about her.

She gives herself to me and then she washes herself with a soft cloth, dipping it into a basin of water. When she's done bathing herself, she splashes perfume over her body. I love watching her. I must remember her favorite fragrance, Violetta de Parma. She loves violets.

We don't spend enough time with each other. But we have to be careful. What would people think if they knew about our affair? As we lie there together, looking up at the ceiling, she asks me if I am afraid of death. Why is she philosophical? I tell her I can deal with death if I finish what I set out to do, to be a great painter. Is that all you want? she asks. And you, I tell her.

What is death? Dying was agonizing for my father and Charles. I loved talking with Charles and hearing his voice reciting his poetry. Will his poetry live on? He's been gone for two years now. I don't think he was afraid of death. Delacroix has been gone for seven years. He was such a brilliant painter. I wonder how he faced death.

Berthe asks me if I believe in God. I tell her I'm not sure. It's something I don't think much about.

I avoid asking her the same questions. I ask if she's materialistic. Are you calling me bourgeois? she asks. Maybe you are, she adds. I like nice things, but I'm not; I tell her. She says she's not, but adds she wants a husband to buy her nice things. I want her to be happy, but I can't give up my family.

We get out of the bed, and she dresses. She will have to leave for home. She's looking a little thinner today. I worry about her health. We can hear the shells falling, but luckily, they are not that close today. She will be safe in the carriage. All I care about is that she is safe.

I put my uniform back on. Berthe tells me I spend a lot of time changing into and out of it. My military knapsack has my paint box and easel in it. I haven't painted anything yet, but having it reminds me what's important.

We hope to get through this without a scratch. Berthe tells me all of this has been a nightmare, except for the time we are together, and it amazed her she has been so strong.

I worry about her safety. If anything were to happen to her, I don't know what I would do.

Chapter Thirty-One

Seven years went by before Julian saw Marlene again. He often wondered what happened to her until early one morning in October 1870. It was the day Nadar sent up his first balloon to carry the mail out of Paris.

There was no way to get the mail through the Prussian lines. Nadar organized some of his friends to create the First Balloon Company. In the beginning, Nadar only made observation flights to plot the various positions of the Prussians and dropped propaganda leaflets over the troops. But that had little value for the French government, which he later convinced to allow the mail to be carried by balloons out of Paris.

That morning, Édouard and Julian went to see Nadar. As they approached Nadar, who was standing in a giant field at the Place Saint- Pierre, preparing the balloon he called Neptune to go up, they saw a young woman standing next to him. Julian was more than surprised to see that it was Marlene.

"What a beautiful morning," Nadar said, puffing on a cigar.

"Yes, it is," Julian said as he walked up to Marlene.

"Hello, Julian," she said. "Good morning, Édouard."

"Is it really you, Marlene?" Julian said.

"Yes."

"Where have you been?"

"In England, studying."

"I didn't know where she had gone after she quit," Nadar said. "Then I was shocked when she came to see me just days ago."

Julian had a bewildered look on his face "Studying what for six years?" Julian asked.

"Don't give her a hard time," Édouard said. "Aren't you glad to see her? You've talked about her so many times."

"Yes, of course I'm glad. But what were you studying? "Julian asked, taking her aside so that they could be alone to talk. She looked the same as the day she left, only a little thinner, but still beautiful in Julian's eyes.

"We're going to catch up with each other," Julian said, as they continued to walk away.

"Bring her back soon. She's one of the pilots," Nadar shouted to them as they walked away.

"Why did you leave Paris?" Julian asked.

"I wanted to learn more about photography and ballooning."

"You could have stayed and learned from Nadar."

"I wanted to be on my own. I didn't want to owe anyone anything."

"Why?"

"Because that's who I am."

"You didn't tell me where you were going when you left that morning."

"That's because I met a man from England who had come to Paris a few days before I met you. He was involved with a project, taking photographs from a balloon. He was on his way back to England and needed an assistant. We talked, and he offered to teach me everything he knew about photography and ballooning."

"Like I said, you could have stayed and learned just as much from Nadar."

"And gotten involved with you?"

"Who knows what would have happened?"

"I thought I wasn't ready to get involved, but I'm sorry to say

141

I made a mistake and did get involved with the man from England."

"Where is he now?"

"I don't know. I left him."

"Why?"

"He found another woman. That's probably what would have happened to us."

"How can you be sure?"

"I just knew. I didn't want to find out I was right."

"You didn't stick around to find out."

"I know. I'm sorry."

They walked back to where Édouard and Nadar were standing. Nearly a thousand people had gathered, waiting for the balloon to lift off. Julian noticed another man standing next to Édouard and Nadar.

"Let me introduce you to Pierre Deroof," Nadar said to Marlene. "He's the other pilot."

"A woman pilot," Deroof said, looking at Marlene. "You didn't tell me, Nadar."

"Yes. A woman pilot. I've made many flights," Marlene said.

"How many have you made?" Deroof asked Marlene.

"Several."

"Enough. Enough," Nadar said. "She knows what she is doing. Maybe Deroof, you can learn something from her."

"Thank you, Felix," Marlene said.

"I'm worried about you," Julian said.

"Don't worry about me. I'll be fine."

Deroof loaded the pouches of mail into the balloon's gondola. Nadar loaded several cages with carrier pigeons onto the wicker frame. After the cages had been secured, Marlene climbed up a ladder into the gondola.

"Getting a balloon to drift back to Paris is very difficult," Nadar said. "The pigeons can be used to get messages back."

"How will you get back?" Julian asked Marlene.

"She'll get back," Édouard said.

"I'll come back when I think it's safe," she said.

"That could be weeks, even months," Julian said. "You've got to promise me you'll come back.

"Don't worry. I'll come back."

Julian was feared he might not see Marlene again. Either she might get caught by the Prussians as she tried to return to Paris or she may just decide not to come back. He really didn't know whether he would see her again.

The sun was just coming up over Paris and there was a chill in the air. The soldiers, who had been holding the balloon in place with ropes, let go.

"I'll send a carrier pigeon back with a message once we've landed safely," Marlene shouted.

The crowd watched as the balloon floated up above the city below the clouds.

Chapter Thirty-Two

In early January 1871, Julian and Édouard returned from Champigny, about fifteen miles from Paris, where the French Army had unsuccessfully attempted to disrupt the Prussian army's siege. Thousands of French soldiers crossed the Marne River to break the ring the Prussians had formed around Paris. The battle left thousands dead and wounded and the villages in ruins.

Julian and Edouard were among the men stationed along the barricade around the city. They kept watch for any Prussian soldiers who might attempt to storm the defense. check on. Julian noticed a man with a rifle slung over his shoulder coming toward them.

"Identify yourself," Julian hollered out.

"Don't shoot. It's Pierre Pelleton," the man yelled back.

When the man got close enough for Julian and Édouard to get a good look at him, they were almost in shock. It *was* Pierre Pelleton. Julian and Édouard had not seen him since Gladiateur won the Grand Prix at the Hippodrome. He had stopped coming to Édouard's studio and to the café.

"What are you doing here?" Édouard asked.

"Strange as it may seem, I was looking for you."

'Why were you looking for me?" Édouard asked.

"I thought you might know of someone I could work for doing anything. I'm desperate for work."

"I'm sorry. Many of the people I know who stayed in Paris

are doing what Julian and I are doing. They've given up their regular lives and many are in the National Guard."

"I understand," Pierre said.

"But how did you find us?" Julian asked.

"I met a guardsman who I asked about Edouard. I thought of all the people I know, Édouard might know someone who had work. The guardsman said he knew Édouard and that he was in the same unit."

"What was his name?" Édouard asked.

"I can't remember. But he said if I were looking for you, I might find you along this section of the barricade."

"As usual, that sounds a little difficult to believe," Julian said.

"For now, I'll give Pierre the benefit of the doubt," Édouard said. "Sit down here on the straw."

"Where have you been these last few years?" Julian asked.

"And why did you stop coming to the studio?" Édouard asked.

"I know you're not going to believe this, but I stopped coming to the studio because I met a woman."

"I've heard this story before," Julian said.

"No. It's true, she's a very interesting woman; someone I could talk to. We got to know each other so well that we got married and not too long after that, she had a baby," Pierre said.

"Your baby?" Julian asked

"Yes, my baby."

"Every man needs a family," Édouard said.

"You're right, Édouard That's what I needed."

"How long have you been together?" Julian asked.

"Let me think. About five years."

"You still could have come by the studio," Édouard said.

"I know. Are you still painting?'

"Not as much as I would like because of this damn war," Édouard said. "How are you dealing with it?"

"It's all horrible. That's why I'm looking for any kind of work. I worry about my family every day,"

"I know how that is," Édouard said. "I had to send my wife and Leon away from Paris."

"But in some ways, I've been lucky. Before this terrible war, I was making money sitting for other painters, although they're not as good as you," Pierre said. "That's how I met my wife."

"What do you mean?" Julian asked.

"There was an artist who saw me on the street and asked me to pose for him. He was working on a painting of a man and a woman in each other's arms and he said I was perfect."

"Yes. What happened?" Julian asked."

"When I got to his studio, there she was, Julia."

"How romantic," Julian said, with sarcasm in his voice.

"Romantic. You know a lot more words than I do, Julian, but I know what romantic means," Pierre said.

"What is she like?" Édouard asked.

"She's just what I needed. I look after her and she looks after me," Pierre said.

As Pierre, Édouard, and Julian continued to talk, the shelling around them became more intense.

"When do you think this will all be over?" Pierre asked.

"It's hard to tell, but I'm sick and tired of eating rats and horses for dinner," Julian said.

Suddenly, a single rifle shot rang out and Julian watched Pierre grab his arm.

"What the hell?" Édouard shouted, staring at Pierre's bloody arm. Édouard quickly helped Pierre to the ground. He took off his coat, ripped off his shirt, and twisted it around Pierre's arm. "That should stop the bleeding," Édouard said.

"It isn't that bad," Pierre said.

Julian, who was standing over Pierre, leaned down to look at the arm. "Maybe it isn't bad, but we need to get you to a doctor," Julian said.

"I know a doctor. He's about a mile from here. Can you make it that far?" Édouard asked.

"Yes, I can make it if we walk slowly."

When they got to the doctor's home, Édouard knocked on the front door. They waited for several minutes before the doctor came to the door.

"What's going on?" the doctor asked.

"This man's been shot, and we need you to look at him," Julian said.

The doctor ushered them into a room and took off the bloody shirt wrapped around Pierre's arm "It doesn't look that bad to me. I'll clean it up and put on some clean bandages," the doctor said.

"I'm going to be fine. I have a place," Pierre said. "It's just that I don't know how I'm going to get there."

"I have a carriage and I can get someone to take you," the doctor said.

Chapter Thirty-Three

On January 28, 1871, Paris surrendered to Prussia. For six months, Paris had endured the siege of the city by Prussian soldiers.

The French government negotiated a peace treaty with Prussia. But the people of Paris, angry about how much they had suffered, opposed the French government and established a revolutionary government called the Commune. The opposition resulted in a civil war between the French government and the working-class Parisians. On March 18, the Commune took over the government. A Communal Assembly was elected to administer the city, passing legislation aimed at improving the lives of the poor.

The French Army evacuated the city when two commanding officers were captured and executed. On May 21, with 120,000 soldiers, the Army returned and captured most of Paris by May 29. As they retreated, the Commune soldiers set fire to government buildings, including the Tuileries Palace, the Palace of Justice, and the Hotel de Ville. The Commune also executed the Archbishop of Paris and several other hostages. Before the conflict was over, the French Army executed as many as 25,000 Communards and the Seine literally ran red with blood.

Édouard had left Paris in February so he could join his family at Oloron-Sainte-Marie and came back in late May. When he returned, he and Julian walked the city, horrified by the carnage and destruction. There were still decaying bodies in the streets.

Houses were gutted by fire. The Hotel de la Legion d'Honner, the Orsay barracks, and the Tuileries were in ruins. They examined the holes that pitted the walls of the Louvre from the shells that had struck it and they saw that much of the Rue Royale was demolished.

"This is horrifying. So many deaths and so much destruction," Édouard said.

"It's more than horrifying. I blame Louis-Napoleon and those officials who signed the peace treaty. If I were to write about all this misery, I'd begin with Louis- Napoleon," Julian said, shaking his head.

"I also blame the leaders of the Commune. They don't have clean hands, either. They're just as responsible as Louis-Napoleon and the government. The more I think about it, the more I believe we're all responsible for what happened."

As Édouard and Julian continued their walk, they witnessed a vast column of smoke covering Paris and later in the day, a huge luminous red cloud flooded the sky.

When they came to Édouard's studio on the Rue Pierrot, Édouard threw up his hands as he surveyed the destruction. The walls and roof had fallen in and Julian helped Édouard scavenge through what was left. They found several paintings that could be restored, but a half dozen others were destroyed.

The next day, they took a carriage to Luxembourg Gardens to check on Elizabeth Gardner and her friend. When they arrived, they found Elizabeth picking through several canvases that lay on the ground outside the studio which had been flattened into a heap of broken boards. All around her were burned paintings, some partially and others completely destroyed.

"Are you all right?" Édouard asked. "Is your friend all right?"

"Yes. But many of our paintings were severely damaged," Elizabeth said.

Édouard watched Elizabeth, examine each painting to see how badly it was damaged.

"Do you know how your studio was destroyed?" Julian asked.

"It was a powder magazine the Commune blew up. It damaged many of the buildings in the neighborhood. We were lucky we weren't here when it happened."

"I'm sorry about your paintings, but glad to see you are all right," Julian said.

"Have you seen Berthe?" Elizabeth asked.

"She went to Cherbourg and said she would be back soon," Édouard said.

"I hope she's all right," Elizabeth said, as she put down one canvas with a sad look on her face. "A few can be saved."

"I'm sure Berthe is fine. I'm looking forward to painting her again." Édouard said. "I think I know someone who can help restore your paintings. I'll contact him."

"Thank you, Édouard. I hope to see you and Julian again soon."

They said goodbye to Elizabeth and walked back to the carriage.

"I thought Berthe would be back by now," Édouard said. "I wonder if she's coming back ."

"Be serious. I'm sure she'll be back soon."

The two went to Édouard's apartment. Suzanne was at the piano, and Leon was sitting next to her in a big easy chair and reading a book. Suzanne looked like she had gained even more weight since the last time Julian saw her.

"I guess you're glad to be back in Paris?" Julian said.

"Yes, although it's not the Paris I left."

"No, it's not and I don't know if we'll ever recover," Édouard said.

"I can see you're depressed, Édouard. It's time for you to get back to your work," Suzanne said.

"I don't know."

"You need to start painting again," Julian said. "Why did you bother to rent another studio?"

"Just because I have a studio doesn't mean I have to go back to painting."

"He doesn't sleep at night, Julian."

"You don't need to speak for me," Édouard said.

"You need to see Dr. Sireday as soon as possible," she said. "Édouard collapsed the other day."

"All right, I know I need to see him."

The next day Julian met Édouard at his apartment, and they went to see Dr. Sireday who was Édouard's doctor and a friend of the family.

Dr. Sireday examined Édouard for more than an hour. He said he was concerned about Édouard, but he was general in his diagnosis.

"I think you're suffering from exhaustion. Maybe you need to get out of Paris for a while."

"I think you're right and I'm going to." The next day, Édouard left for Boulogne.

Chapter Thirty-Four

When Édouard returned from Boulogne, Julian met him at the train station. Édouard said he felt better because of his stay in Boulogne and was glad to be back in Paris but he wanted to know if Julian had heard from Pierre.

"No, I haven't talked to him since we left him at that doctor's home eight months ago. Why do you ask?"

"I want him to pose for another painting."

"I don't know why he hasn't contacted us, but I'm sure we can find him."

"How do you propose we do that.?"

"It will be easy. The doctor who treated him should be able to tell us what address the carriage took him to that night"

When Édouard and Julian returned to the doctor's home, he was able to remember the address because it was in one of the poorer sections of Paris.

"The driver repeated the address a couple of times before he left because he was so concerned about going to such a depressed area. But I got the driver to agree to take him," the doctor said.

When Édouard and Julian reached the address and knocked on the door, a petite woman with red hair and freckles opened the door. Standing next to her was a young boy, four or five years old.

"I'm sorry to bother you, Madam, but are you, Julia, Pierre's wife? We're looking for Pierre," Édouard said.

"Yes, I'm Julia. What do you want with Pierre?" she asked.

"I'm a painter and I'm trying to find him and see if he'll pose

152

for a painting I'm working on. He's done it for me before and I'll pay him well."

"Yes. I've heard about you," she said. "Pierre talked about you and your painting of him, the one that the Salon rejected. He was so angry about that."

"So, is he here or do you know where I can find him?" Édouard asked.

"I've got no use for painters, not you nor the one who came here a few days ago."

She looked down at the boy who had reached for her hand. "Go inside, Tommy, and I'll give you your supper," she said and looked at Édouard again.

"All I can tell you is I overheard the man who had come to see Pierre tell him he'd pay him a thousand francs. Imagine, a thousand francs. That's what Pierre and I made in six months posing for artists like you and more than I now make in a year washing clothes."

She turned to go inside and was about to close the door. "I don't know what it was he wanted Pierre to do but I heard him say something about the Salon. A few days later, the police came looking for Pierre. But he had left and I haven't seen him since then," she said.

"Do you think Pierre was paid to kill someone on the Salon jury?" Julian whispered to Édouard.

"I'm not sure. But there are many artists who hold grudges against Salon judges because their paintings have been rejected," Édouard said.

"Excuse me Madame. Did the police say why they wanted to see Pierre?" Julian asked.

"No, of course not."

She slammed the door and Édouard and Julian found themselves on the street.

Chapter Thirty-Five

Nadar's balloon carrying the mail crossed the Prussian lines and landed on the Normandy coast. Marlene sent a message by carrier pigeon to Julian telling him she was safe. But she also told him she needed some time to think and decide what she wanted to do with her life. She told him she was staying in Normandy and would come back to Paris in a month.

During that month, Julian and Marlene wrote to each other. Marlene often wrote she felt an emptiness in her life and that she needed something more. Julian wrote to her that he sometimes felt an emptiness but that when he was writing it would always vanish.

Marlene finally came back to Paris after a month. She went back to work again for Nadar. She immersed herself in photography, taking photographs of the movers and shakers of the time. Julian wanted to rekindle what he thought they once had. But he couldn't erase from his mind the emptiness Marlene said she felt. Maybe he couldn't fill her emptiness, but she was the only woman he wanted.

At first, he didn't try to see her, but a month after she returned, he asked her to dinner. Never quite understanding her, he was surprised when she said yes.

They met at the Café Anglaise. She was once again flawlessly beautiful, wearing a white dress that glowed around her. When she saw Julian, she had an immense smile on her face. He pulled her chair out so she could sit down. As he did, the fragrance of lavender drifted over him and the memory of them together. "Good evening, Marlene. You look beautiful tonight," Julian said.

"Thank you, Julian. I think you look very nice."

The restaurant was noisy, and filled with lawyers, artists, and writers. There were several people Julian knew. One of them, a lawyer, walked over to their table.

"Good evening, Monsieur Semrad," Julian said, speaking loudly so he could be heard over the noise of the people at the tables around them.

Semrad looked at Julian and then smiled at Marlene. "What a lovely lady," he said.

"Thank you, Monsieur," Marlene said.

"I used to come to this restaurant often," he said.

"You don't anymore?" Julian said.

"Not that often."

"That's too bad. They have the best oysters."

"Yes, I know, and the salmon mayonnaise is excellent. You should try it," Semrad said.

"Maybe we'll take your advice."

"I'm sorry but I need to get back to my table. Enjoy your evening."

"Who was that?" Marlene asked as the waiter came to their table with their menus. They were bound in leather and twenty pages thick. "How nice," she said.

"His name is Antoine Semrad, and he stinks of confidence because he's the lawyer who defended Flaubert over his novel, *Madame Bovary*."

"Why would you say he stinks of confidence?"

"I'm sorry. I shouldn't have said it. It's because I worry about my stuttering, a problem he's never had, I'm sure. I don't think as much about it as I used to. The older I get, the less it happens. I've always wondered why you never said anything about it to me."

"That's because I hardly noticed it and I would never say anything about it."

"Thank you. That's what I like about you."

"So, what about Monsieur Semrad and Madame Bovary?"

"He defended Flaubert on the morality charges and was successful."

"Would you be surprised if I told you I've read the novel?"

"No. I wouldn't be. I've read it twice, hoping to learn something from the way Flaubert writes about his characters."

"Do you read every novel twice?"

"Not every novel. "

"I'm glad to hear that. Maybe you could learn something by reading it just once."

"Maybe. By the way, I think Flaubert's lawyer is now the Mayor of St. Cloud."

"Why do you know that?"

"It's part of my job as a journalist. You need to know people and know about them."

"What do you know about Monsieur Flaubert's Emma in *Madame Bovary*? Did you feel bad for her?"

"I'm not sure."

'You're not sure? I felt bad for her because women who cheat on their husbands are looked down on, while men who cheat on their wives get away with it."

"I agree with you. Then yes, I do feel bad for her."

"I'm glad to hear that. But it did bother me that she looked at marriage as a life of adventure."

"And then she grew bored and unhappy being married."

"I wouldn't be bored or be unhappy being married."

156

"You wouldn't? You've thought about it?"

"Yes. I've thought about it."

Julian noticed the waiter had returned to take their orders and asked him how long he had been standing there.

"Not long, sir."

Marlene whispered to Julian. "Do you think he overheard some of our conversation?"

"I don't think he did, and I wouldn't worry about it."

"That makes me feel better."

Julian looked up at the waiter. "Can we have some more time?"

"Yes. Take all the time you need. I'll come back."

"Do you think he was being funny with us?" Marlene asked.

"What do you mean?"

"I'm sure he did hear us talking about marriage and that's why he told us to take all the time we needed."

"I'm sure he was just talking about us deciding on what we wanted for dinner."

"All right," Marlene said, looking down at her menu. "I don't know what I want."

"Take your time because I think first, we should order some wine." Julian waved at the waiter, who came back to the table.

"We'd like some wine, a bottle of Chateau Margaux."

The waiter left and within minutes returned with the wine. He uncorked the bottle and poured a small amount for Julian to taste.

"Perfect, Julian said, after quickly swirling it around in his mouth "

"You've got excellent taste," the waiter said, as he wrote down what they wanted for dinner and headed for the kitchen.

"What do you think he meant by excellent taste? Was he

talking about the wine or you," Julian said smiling.

"Me, of course."

"The waiter will be gone for a while. In the meantime, I want to ask you something."

"What?"

"Why haven't we seen that much of each other since you got back?"

"I didn't know you cared."

"It bothers me."

"It shouldn't."

"Do you enjoy being with me?"

"Yes. Of course, I do."

"I just wanted to hear you say it."

"You know about the emptiness I sometimes feel."

"I know, but everyone feels empty once in a while."

"I know and it doesn't happen that often any more. Being back at Nadar's studio has helped. I'm excited about my work. Just a few weeks ago I had one of the greatest moments."

"What was that?"

"Taking a photograph of Jules Verne. You know the novelist who wrote *Five Weeks in a Balloon*."

"Yes. I've read it. I like adventure. In fact, I'd like to go back to Brazil. I went there when I was sixteen."

"I know and you and Édouard were cadets on a ship. What was Édouard, like back then?"

"Why do you ask?"

"He's so difficult to understand."

"Back then, he was driven, just as he is today. He wanted to be a painter when I met him and I knew he was going to be a great one someday."

"Yes. It's easy to see he's driven. And I agree with you he's going to be a great artist."

"All the years I've known him, he's also had an unpredictable side, but I think that's the nature of many artists."

"Maybe. But enough about Édouard. I want you to tell me more about Rio."

"After all the years, I still have a vivid memory of going ashore and exploring the city. I'll never forget entering the harbor and gliding alongside the other ships and the gray granite mountain tops that were all around us."

"You make me want to go there."

"Would you settle for Trouville? I've been thinking about asking you to go with me next week.

It's not Rio, but it's a beautiful city. Would you like to go with me?"

"Yes, I'll go. I think we need to get to know each other better.

Chapter Thirty-Six

The train was filling up quickly as Marlene and Julian boarded, took their seats, and then watched the other passengers get on. Many of the passengers brought trunks that needed to be stored at either end of the cars.

Julian watched one man get on whom he thought he recognized. He was carrying several small canvases and walked to the end of the car where he stacked them in a section used to store luggage.

"I think I know that man with the canvases," Julian whispered to Marlene. "He looks a lot like Ernest Meissonier. You know, the rich painter whose work is so much different than Édouard's."

"I noticed him too because I was watching another man who seemed to be following him."

"Why did you think he was being followed?"

"Because every few feet, the man I was watching would step out of the aisle and into the nearest vacant seat. He kept doing that until the man with the canvases sat down."

"What did he look like?"

"You're going to find this hard to believe but he looked a lot like the man in Édouard 's painting The Absinthe Drinker."

"You could be right. Ever since that day, Pierre met Meissonier, I've been worried."

"Why have you been worried."

"While Édouard may say I'm wrong, I think Pierre may want

160

to murder Meissonier."

"Why?"

"Because he has been a Salon judge and has voted against Édouard 's paintings."

Maybe I'm wrong and the man I saw wasn't following the man you think looked like Meissonier."

"When we get to Trouville, I'll watch for the two men when we get off the train."

Julian and Marlene spent most of the five-hour train ride talking. A few times Julian got up and walked through the train to see if Meissonier or Pierre were on it, but he didn't see them. When they reached the station, Julian grabbed their bags, exited the train, and stood on the platform with Marlene.

"If we don't see Meissonier or Pierre get off, then I guess we were wrong, and they weren't on the train. Anyway, I like watching the people as they get off the train."

"So, you like to watch people?"

"Yes. You can learn a lot about people just by watching them."

"Like what?"

"Sometimes you can tell if they're happy or sad. If you see that they take their time to enjoy the moment, then there's a good chance they're happy."

"What if they're in a rush?"

"Then, maybe they're not so happy."

"So, what do you do with these observations?"

"Sometimes I write them down in a journal I keep."

They watched as the conductor began unloading the crates that contained the pets many of the passengers had brought with them. There were at least two monkeys, three parrots, and several dogs. As she watched, Marlene had a hard time not laughing.

After waiting around for an hour to see if Meissonier or Pierre had been on the train they gave up and got into a carriage to their hotel.

"What a beautiful place, but the town has such an unusual name. I don't think I've ever been here before or I would have remembered the name." Marlene said.

"It is unusual. It's from the Norse word, Thoruflr, which literally means Thor's wolf. The Vikings got here long before us and then left. Hopefully, the wolves are gone too,"

"You're quite the historian."

"Thank you. What else do you have to say about me?"

"You're very nice. That's why I came with you."

Julian reached out to hold Marlene's hand.

"Hey, stranger," he said, trying to make light of holding her hand.

"I'm no stranger. Don't you remember those five days and nights we spent together?"

"Yes. I've got a good memory of it."

"I would hope you remembered."

"But not the morning you left."

"I'm sorry, Julian."

"I know."

They checked into the hotel and went up to their room to unpack. A vase of daisies stood on a table in the corner of the room and Julian reached for one and gave it to Marlene.

"You're very forward," she said with a smile.

"I…I- guess…. I am…. with you." Julian said.

"That's all right."

They spent the afternoon walking along the silvery white beach and watching the sailboats gliding through the waves. At sunset, they watched the pink clouds gradually become gray. Some clouds dispersed, and the sky got bluer. They watched until

162

the sun went below the horizon and then they walked slowly back to the hotel.

Once back in their room Marlene closed the door and stood looking at Julian.

"Will you help me get undressed?" Marlene asked.

"Yes."

After they had helped each other get undressed, Julian quickly lifted Marlene and carried her to bed.

Lying next to each other, they held each other's hands, their fingers on fire. Then he kissed her around her ear and down her neck. His hand drifted to her breasts, and he caressed them. Slowly he moved his mouth to her nipples, his tongue circling them, one at a time.

"That makes me feel warm inside," she said. "Keep me warm."

She stretched her legs open. Julian couldn't wait any longer. He moved down her body to the warmth between her legs. "Keep going some more," she said. Her voice became softer and softer.

"Are you mine?" he asked.

"Yes. I'm yours," she murmured. "I want all of you."

Chapter Thirty-Seven

On July 1, 1872, Édouard moved into a new studio on Rue de Saint-Pétersbourg. It was a vast ground-floor studio with four large windows. The interior had oak paneling, high ceilings, and a roofed gallery. It was furnished with a piano, a garden bench, a console table, and a mirror. There was also a table for dining with several chairs. The walls were covered with paintings.

From July through the autumn of 1872, Édouard painted four portraits of Berthe, spending many hours with her. Julian visited Édouard one afternoon a few weeks after he had moved into the studio and Berthe was there.

"I asked Berthe to model for me again," Édouard said. "Don't you think her face is stunning?"

"Yes. She has a very beautiful face," Julian said, his face turning red, looking embarrassed. Berthe was standing in front of him.

For a moment Julian smiled at her and then he knew he should change the subject. "Have you heard anything more about Pierre?" Julian asked Édouard.

"No, nothing more since you and Marlene told me you saw someone who looked like him on a train to Trouville and that he was following another man who you thought could have been Ernest Meissonier."

"Yes, that was strange. We didn't see either one of them get off the train. So, we think we were probably wrong."

"Maybe. I didn't think it was worth it to say anything to

Meissonier when I saw him." The red in Julian's face had slowly disappeared, and he no longer felt embarrassed talking to Berthe.

"So, when did you get here?" he asked.

"Early this morning."

Julian didn't know whether he should believe her. A blanket was spread over the crimson sofa and two cushions were on the floor. It looked like someone had been sleeping there.

"How was your trip from Passy?"

"Very nice. I'm captivated by the tree-lined streets."

"Thanks to Monsieur Haussmann," Julian said halfheartedly.

"Paris could be worse off, "Berthe said.

Édouard told Julian he was working on a painting with Berthe sitting in a chair holding a Spanish fan, but it didn't look like he had started. An easel with a blank canvas was standing in one corner of the room.

"You haven't begun?"

"Not yet. Berthe got here for breakfast and then we started talking and you know how time flies."

"We'll start today," Berthe quickly said.

"I'd love to see it when it's finished," Julian said.

Édouard went to the other corner of the room where his canvases were stacked, picked one up, and set it on the easel. Then he grabbed his palette and squirted out some paint from a few of the tubes laying on a stand next to the easel.

"Now, I can start painting. Are you ready Berthe?" Édouard asked. Berthe hurried into an adjoining room and came back minutes later wearing an alluring black dress.

Chapter Thirty-Eight

It was a cold January evening in 1873 when Édouard celebrated Leon's twenty-first birthday at the Folies-Bergère.

The cabaret music hall had a theater, an indoor garden, a bar, and a promenade. An area next to the theater was lined with tables. People drank and mingled in the garden and promenade area and enjoyed performances in the theater. Those performances often included acrobats, snake charmers, boxing kangaroos, and elephants. Sometimes the entertainment was an opera or ballet.

Julian and Nadar accompanied Édouard and Leon to the Folies-Bergère. They stood at the bar while Édouard ordered beers for the four of them.

A tall blonde barmaid with bright blue eyes who was standing behind the bar reached for the glasses. Julian thought she was young, probably Leon's age. She placed the glasses on the bar, got four bottles of beer, opened them, and slowly filled each glass.

Leon seemed mesmerized watching her as she filled each glass. When she was finished pouring, Édouard lifted his glass high in the air. Nadar, Leon, and Julian did the same.

"Here's to you, Leon," Édouard said. "It's a big day for you."

"Yes, it is, sir. Thank you," Leon said.

Julian noticed Leon never used Édouard's first name when talking to him. It was always sir. As weak a reason as it was, it was one of the many that made Julian think Leon was Édouard's son. Édouard and Suzanne seemed very much like father and mother. And Leon had many of Édouard 's features, especially his eyes. But Édouard would introduce Leon as his godson and Suzanne's brother.

As the four men stood at the bar, they watched the men and women hurry into the theater, dressed up, the men with their top hats and frock coats and the women with their flowing dresses and bright jewelry.

"Did you see that one?" Nadar said, looking at one woman. "Her breasts are almost pushing out from her dress."

"No, I didn't," Leon said. I'm sorry I missed her." Julian saw why he missed her; Leon's eyes were on the barmaid.

"What's your name?" Leon asked the barmaid.

"Lily, like the flower," she said.

"That's a pretty name."

"Thank you. That's nice of you to say.

"So, what's it like working here? Do you enjoy it?"

"Yes. Very much. What do you do?"

I'm working at a bank as a clerk but someday I want to be a writer."

"I meet so many men who say they want to be a writer just to impress the woman they are talking to.

"That's a harsh thing for you to say. I'm telling you the truth."

Édouard heard some of the conversation and interrupted.

"It's true. He wants to be a writer and writes at night when he gets home from his job at the bank," Édouard said. "He's a very hard-working young man."

"Who are you? "Lily asked.

"I'm his godfather."

"You know he's a painter," Leon said proudly.

167

"He is?" she said. "What's his name?"

"Manet. Édouard Manet."

"Oh, the artist who paints naked women."

"What are you talking about?" Nadar asked.

"About Édouard. She's heard of him," Leon said.

"Did you tell her who I am?" Nadar asked.

"No. Do you want me to?"

The bar area was getting smokier, with many of the men lighting up cigars.

"Have you ever modeled?" Leon asked Lily.

"No, I haven't."

"You look like you'd make an excellent model."

"But I know a woman who has modeled."

"Who?"

"The woman singing tonight."

"You mean Vanessa?"

"Yes, her."

"That's why we're here tonight. We wanted to see her."

"Well, you'll see a lot of her. She doesn't wear much."

"Is she good?"

"The men seem to think so."

"Do you think she's good?"

"Not at singing," Lily said with a smile. People started leaving the bar and headed for the theater.

"It's about time we get our seats," Édouard said. "We don't want to miss anything."

"No, we don't," Julian said.

"I'm eager to see her," Nadar said.

"Maybe I'll see you later," Leon said to Lily.

"Maybe," she said.

Édouard, Nadar, Leon, and Julian quickly strode into the

theater. They had just gotten to their seats when the curtain came up.

Standing on the stage was a woman. She's certainly voluptuous, Julian thought. Most of her costume was jewelry, nothing more. Then she opened her mouth to sing. Many of the men stood up to clap. Some of the women in the audience looked on in awe.

Édouard, Julian, Nadar, and Leon stood up to clap, even though her voice sounded awful. It was an irritating and screechy voice, but that didn't seem to bother many of the men in the audience.

"I'd rather be back at the bar," Leon said.

"I would, too," Édouard said.

"Then, let's go," Julian said.

"I'm going to stay to stay and listen to her sing," Nadar said. "I'll meet you after the performance."

The bar was nearly empty. Lily was talking to a man, a little older than her. As Édouard ordered drinks, the man left.

"Who's he?" Leon asked.

"He's my brother," Lily said.

"Oh. I shouldn't have asked."

"So, did you like Vanesa's singing?"

"No. The men think she's good, but not for her singing."

"Why didn't you stay?"

"Because I wanted to come back and see you." Édouard said.

"Why?"

"Because I find you very attractive," Leon said.

"Oh."

Leon and Lily talked for more than an hour until Nadar came back to the bar.

"We better be on our way," Leon said. "I hope to see you again."

"I do too," Lily said.

As they walked to get a carriage, Édouard smiled at Leon.

"Have you found your muse?" Édouard asked.

"Maybe," Leon said.

Chapter Thirty-Nine

Édouard Manet's Journal
January 30, 1873

Leon celebrated his twenty-first birthday at the Folies-Bergère. He's in love with the barmaid. I can see why. She's very beautiful. I wonder how much Leon is like me. Does he think he'll live forever? Will he see the world as I do, through the eyes of a twenty-one-year-old, for the rest of his life? I wonder if he will be as ambitious as I am.

I'm troubled that I've never told Leon he's my son and Suzanne is his mother. All these years, I've said I'm his godfather and Suzanne is his sister. How could we have done that? I wonder what people think. Do they believe the myth we have created? They've never questioned me. It isn't their concern.

We were afraid to accept responsibility. What would my mother and father think? What would Suzanne's family think? We were wrong. Some say Leon should have been baptized right after he was born But I disdain any religious observance, and I don't know if I believe in God.

The closest I have come to religion are my paintings of Christ. Christ on the cross. What a symbol. One could rack one's brains till the end of time and find nothing like it. No image can ever equal the image of suffering. This is the basis of humanity.

I would not have been the godfather of a child by another man. Are people stupid? Did I benefit from that stupidity?

171

What has this done to Leon? What has it done to Suzanne? What has it done to me? How has it changed my life? I've been able to know I have a family without taking responsibility for having a son. Leon's existence has been a fabric of lies. What is it worth? Would he be angry if I told him now?

I feel guilty about not loving Suzanne as much as a husband should. Is that because she is no longer as attractive as she once was or because of our secret?

Sometimes I tire of her asking me if I still love her. I have to answer yes. I could never tell her not as much. I'm afraid she would go back to Holland and take Leon. I would no longer have a family, and family is so important to me.

Berthe excites me when she gives herself. We are serious about our lovemaking. She will lie in the bed while I just look at her beauty. I don't think she has been with another man, but I have never asked her. I would not want to know. She would know that I was jealous. It is enough that she loves me. But I must accept that one day she will marry. It will break my heart. I will have to hide it. I wouldn't want her to see that in my eyes.

Chapter Forty

Leon and Julian went with Édouard to the Masked Opera Ball one day in March 1873. Édouard took out his sketch pad and penciled in the figures of the men and women standing in front of him. More than 200 people were crowded into the ballroom.

Some women wore costumes. All wore elegant masquerade masks that covered their faces. The men were well-dressed with top hats. It seemed like it was the rule for the Salle Le Pelletier Masked Ball. It was an annual rite held from the middle of December until Lent every Saturday evening. The event was held in anticipation of what many of those attending would give up in March when Lent began.

Theater boxes with masked onlookers surrounded the ballroom, and the smell of perfume was everywhere. There were dozens of couples, men, and women, talking to each other. And there was laughter.

Leon and Julian stood next to Édouard as they watched him sketch. Despite the cold weather, the ballroom was warm. Édouard was immersed in his work. Leon was looking at one particular woman.

"Isn't that the woman from the Folies Bergère, Lily?" Leon asked.

"It's hard to tell because of the mask," Julian said.

Leon tapped Édouard on the shoulder. Édouard turned around to look at Leon.

"Do you see that woman next to the other one dressed as a

harlequin?" Leon said. "Isn't she the woman from the Folies-Bergère?"

"I don't know," Édouard said. "She's just as attractive."

"Yes, she is," Leon said. "I wonder if she's here for the same reason many other women come."

"What's that?"

"Don't kid me. You know. Many of the women are here looking for men."

"Not all," Édouard said. "Maybe Lily is just looking for some excitement."

Leon strained his neck to get a better look at the woman.

"I'm sure that's Lily. She looks just like her," he said.

"Go over and talk to her. Then you'll know," Édouard said.

Julian followed Leon as he pushed his way through the crowd. It had gotten smoky from all the cigars many of the men were puffing on. When Leon got to the woman, he smiled at her.

"Excuse me," Leon said. "Aren't you Lily? Didn't we meet at the Folies Bergère?"

"Yes. I remember you. Do you come to the ball every year?"

"No, this is my first time. I came with my godfather. He's working on a painting."

"Yes. Édouard Manet. I remember."

The ballroom was getting louder and more crowded. A woman dressed as a harlequin brushed up against Leon.

"Hello," she said.

"She seems to like you," Lily said.

Leon pulled back from the woman. "Not interested," he said.

"Suit yourself," she said, walking away.

"Not interested?" Lily said.

"Not at all. Who would dress up like a harlequin?"

"You can see there are a lot of women who did."

"Would you?"

174

"No." Julian said. He could hear someone shouting in the far corner of the ballroom. There was a man about twenty feet away shouting.

"That's my wife," the man shouted. He was waving a pistol in the air.

Lily looked across the ballroom. She had a worried look on her face.

"I think that's my brother, and that's his wife," Lily said. "She's probably been flirting with another man. She does that all the time."

"Is your brother dangerous?" Leon asked.

"When it comes to his wife, he can be jealous."

"Don't," the woman standing in front of the man shouted. The man was waving a pistol at her. Another man who had been standing beside the woman quickly moved behind her. Lily ran to the man with the pistol, and Leon followed.

"Put the pistol down, Peter," Lily said.

"I'm going to kill them both," the man said.

"Killing them won't help," Lily said.

"Yes, it will," he said.

The woman the man had pointed the gun at began to cry.

"She's not worth it," Lily said. "Come on, give me the pistol."

The man was silent for a minute. Then he reached out his hand with the pistol. Leon had worked his way behind him and grabbed the pistol. It went off, and a bullet penetrated the floor. The man looked down and then ran, fleeing the ballroom.

"You're a hussy," Lily said to the woman who was her brother's wife. "And you're scum," she said to the man standing behind her.

Édouard had managed to come over and watch what was going on. "You two could have gotten killed," Édouard said.

175

"I didn't want Lily to get hurt," Leon said.

Lily walked over to Leon and gave him a kiss on the cheek.

"I don't know," Lily said.

Édouard and Julian walked back to where Édouard had dropped his sketch pad.

"What do you think of Leon? He asked Julian.

"I think he was very brave."

"Or stupid, but I'm proud of him."

They both looked toward the spot where Lily and Leon had been standing, but they were gone.

For the next several months, Leon saw Lily almost every night. One day in November, Leon brought Lily around to Édouard's studio. He asked Suzanne to be there, too.

Suzanne rushed up to greet them as they walked into the studio. Édouard was at his easel with a brush in hand, working on a painting.

"What have you two been up to?" Suzanne asked.

Édouard looked up from his easel. "Yes. What have you been doing?" he asked.

"That's why we're here. We've got something to tell you," Leon said. "I'm giving up on becoming a writer. I'm certainly not as committed as someone like your friend Julian. I've also learned there is something more important than writing. I've got a good job at the bank."

At that moment, Lily jumped in to speak. "And we're going to get married and have a family. It's something we both want very much."

Édouard put his brush down and walked over to Leon. He put one arm around Leon and the other around Lily. "What do you think of that?" he said to Suzanne.

"I think it's time Leon figured that out," she said. "I'm happy for the two of you."

Chapter Forty-One

Édouard's studio on Rue Saint-Petersburg was a stone's throw from the Gare Saint Lazare train station. Clouds of steam from the trains filled the air. The ground around the station constantly shook, trembling beneath the feet of anyone who stood there. A tunnel swallowed up the trains as they entered the station and an iron grating surrounded it. Beyond the station was the Rue de Rome, with its garden apartments and towering houses.

Julian went to the studio one day to see how Édouard's painting of the train station, was coming. However, the train station was not the focus of the painting. It was only the background. The focal point was a pair of individuals, a woman seated on a bench and a young girl standing in front of a grated fence.

When Julian arrived, Édouard was busy positioning Victorine, the model who posed for "Olympia" and "The Luncheon on the Grass." She was seated fully dressed on a bench in the studio, looking out and holding a small dog and a book in her lap. A little girl with her back to Édouard was standing next to Victorine.

Julian walked up to Victorine and gave her a kiss on the cheek. "Who's the little girl?" he asked.

"She's the daughter of an artist who lives not far from here. Her name is Susan," Édouard said.

Julian smiled at the girl. "Hello, Susan."

"Good morning, sir."

"What do you think of the painting?" Édouard asked.

Julian walked over to the easel to get a better look at it. "How did you go about painting that background? I'm fascinated."

"I painted it standing in front of the grating surrounding the station, looking down."

"The foreground you've been painting in the studio? It looks like you're nearly done."

"I'm hoping to finish it today."

"I hope so too," Victorine said. "I'm getting tired of sitting."

"What do you think of Victorine posing for me again? She was in America for a while."

Julian looked at Victorine. "What made you go to America?"

"I needed to get away from Paris."

"What for?"

"Because I got tired of people stopping to stare at me. If that wasn't enough, some of them would come up to me and say I was the naked woman. It made me feel dirty and ugly."

"That's just the way some people are. They would never hold up a mirror and take a good look at themselves."

"You never told me that," Édouard said.

"I never thought I had to. You know what they've said about some of your paintings, that you've painted a prostitute."

Julian walked over to Susan. She looked like she was listening to every one of Victorine's words. "You two need to talk. I'll take Susan home. Where does she live?"

"You don't have to leave," Édouard said.

"I think there are things you and Victorine need to talk about that someone shouldn't hear," Julian said, looking at Susan.

"You're right. I'll write down the address for you." Édouard said. He had stopped painting, grabbed a piece of paper lying on a table near the easel and wrote down the address for Julian.

"It was good to see you, Victorine. By the way, I think you're beautiful," Julian said as he walked out of the studio to take Susan home.

Chapter Forty-Two

Nadar and Julian arrived at Édouard 's studio early one afternoon in December 1873. Nadar had asked Julian to try and convince Édouard to participate in an independent exhibit.

The exhibit was organized by a group of painters, many Édouard knew. They met on a regular basis at the Café de Nouvelle. It was at the café de Nouvelle that they would talk about painting, writing, and politics. Sometimes it got loud as they drank a few more beers or another carafe of wine, but it was usually friendly conversation. Édouard had gained the respect and even admiration of many of the painters and some of the writers who frequented the café.

When Nadar and Julian arrived at the studio, Édouard opened the door and ushered them in.

"It's good to see you two," Édouard said as he went to his easel. He was working on a painting of a woman dressed in a low-cut gown and wearing a velvet choker that accentuated her dark hair and dark brown eyes.

"Is that Mademoiselle Morisot?" Julian asked. "It's a beautiful painting."

"Yes. She is beautiful," Édouard said.

Nadar walked over to the easel and bent over to get a better look at the painting. "It's very good, Édouard. It's almost like a photograph. "

"Thank you, Felix," Édouard said. "I know you prefer Nadar, but when I really want to thank you, Felix, sound better."

"You can call me Felix today, Édouard."

"Why today?"

"Because I want to ask you to do something."

"What's that?"

"I want you to show some of your paintings at the exhibit at my studio."

"Felix believes in those painters," Julian said. "And so do you, Édouard."

Nadar quickly interjected, with a smile on his face. "I told Édouard he could call me Felix today. I didn't mean everyone."

"All right," Julian grinned.

Julian looked out the window and watched a light snow falling. The flakes stuck to the window for a moment and then slowly slid down the glass, turning into drops of rain.

"I wonder if it will snow all day," Édouard said, trying to change the subject.

"Forget about the snow," Nadar said. "Those painters need a chance to exhibit. They're not getting that chance with the Salon. You know that as well as anyone."

"I'm still against the idea of an independent exhibit," Manet said.

"Why?" Julian asked.

"It's about the success you get from the Salon. I won't jeopardize my chances by exhibiting at an independent show."

"Édouard. You've been rejected so many times," Julian said.

"When you exhibit at the Salon, you get the public's attention," Édouard said. "And it's where the dealers go."

"But the independent exhibit will get the attention of the critics and dealers," Nadar said.

"You know Claude Monet, whom the public sometimes confuses with you, thinks the independent exhibit will help

180

promote the works of everyone who takes part," Julian said.

"You don't need to remind me of the people confusing me with Monet," Édouard said. "And I don't know how successful the exhibit will be."

"You should know your friend Edgar Degas has invited Berthe Morisot to exhibit," Nadar said. "He's sure she will participate."

"I don't think she will," Édouard said. There was a worried look on his face. "It's true the Salon rejected her work this year, but she's been accepted before."

"Well. Think about it," Nadar said. "You're letting the other painters down if you don't."

Julian thought back to earlier in the year when two of Édouard's paintings had been accepted by the Salon. One was a painting of a ruddy bearded man with a clay pipe in one hand and a glass of beer in the other. It was so successful that photographic reproductions of the painting went on sale in all the book shops. The other one was a painting of Berthe Morisot sitting on a sofa in a white summer dress. With those successes, Julian could not understand why Édouard was so much against participating in the independent exhibit with his friends.

"You had a good year," Julian said, "but you know you can't always count on the Salon."

"I have to," Édouard said.

Chapter Forty-Three

Édouard and Julian got into a carriage on their way to Nadar's building. It was a red two-story building with immense glass windows. Nadar's name in ten-foot-tall red gaslit letters stretched across the front of the building. Nadar had agreed to let the Anonymous Society of Painters use his studio for the exhibition.

"I want to see what it will look like," Édouard said.

He still had not agreed to participate in the exhibition despite Nadar's, Julian's, and Berthe's efforts to change his mind.

"I'm going to support these artists but I'm not going to exhibit my work, "Édouard said.

"These are your friends. They look up to you," Julian said. "It doesn't make any sense, Édouard."

"It does to me," Édouard said. "The Salon is the only place I care to exhibit. That is where you build your reputation as an artist."

"The Salon has rejected your work so many times. You should exhibit with these artists whom you respect."

When they reached the studio, on the second floor of the building, Nadar, wearing a red velvet robe greeted them.

"I thought you only wore that when having guests over for dinner," Julian said.

"This is a special occasion," Nadar said. "Have you changed your mind, Édouard?"

"No. I haven't, but I am here to show my support."

Two of the artists, Edgar Degas and Paul Cezanne, part of

the group of artists who founded the cooperative to sponsor the exhibition, stood next to Nadar. They had also sworn, as did the rest of the artists who made up the cooperative, not to participate in the 1874 Salon.

"Édouard and Julian, I'm glad you've come," Degas said.

"I'm glad to be here, but don't waste your time trying to convince me I should exhibit," Édouard said.

A short skinny man was up on a ladder, busy hanging paintings on the striking blood-red walls of the studio. The sun shining through the skylights above produced a bright feeling. The man hanging the paintings had several sheets of paper in his hand that detailed where each painting should be hung. They were to be hung in two rows, with the larger ones above and the smaller ones below. The artists had drawn lots for hanging positions.

Nadar gave Édouard a copy of the exhibition catalog. The catalog introduction confirmed that there were fifty-one artists participating and 200 paintings. Édouard slowly thumbed through it, reading the names of the artists and their works.

"Very impressive," Édouard said.

"We could quickly print up another page with your name and your works and insert it into the catalog," Nadar said with a smile.

"You can't take no for an answer. Can you?" Édouard said. "It's still no, but thank you."

"You're welcome," Nadar said, again with a smile.

"I understand Monet has submitted a painting he calls "Impression Sunrise," Édouard said.

"I heard it was a painting of a sunrise over Le Havre," Julian said.

"Le Havre," Édouard said, with a yearning look on his face. "I have loved Le Havre ever since Julian and I shipped out from there."

"Yes," Julian said.

The exhibition would open in two days, April 15, 1874, just before the Salon in May. Édouard had submitted two paintings to the 1874 Salon. "Ball at the Opera" was rejected, while "The Railroad" was accepted. As they watched the paintings being hung, Julian heard a faint voice, "Édouard."

It was Berthe Morisot. She had just walked into the studio carrying an umbrella, her head covered by a tiny black bonnet.

"Have you seen my painting?" she said, looking directly at Édouard.

"No, not yet," Édouard said. "As always, you are beautiful."

"You don't have to say that."

Julian looked at Berthe, wondering if she could convince Édouard to exhibit.

She shook the umbrella, which was wet from the rain, walked over to a corner of the room and put it against the wall.

"I like the sound of the rain against the windows," Julian said.

"I do too," Berthe said. "But there was a downpour for a few minutes just before I got to the studio, which wasn't so nice."

Berthe took off her rain-soaked bonnet and handed it to Édouard, who shook it a few times to try and dry it out.

"I see your painting is listed as 'The Cradle,'" he said.

"Yes. It's a painting of my sister Edam's newborn. I'm very proud of it."

"You're not going to exhibit at the Salon this year?" Édouard asked.

"No. We all agreed not to submit this year and show our works at the exhibition here," she said.

"But my friend, Elizabeth, the American, had two paintings accepted."

"That's good. It sounds like Mademoiselle Gardner is doing very well."

"I still don't understand why you won't show your paintings at our exhibition," Berthe said.

"Even if it's a success, there's more for me to gain by taking the conventional route – even if *that* sometimes means rejection."

"I think you're making a mistake," Berthe said as she reached to take her bonnet from Édouard. "This is one time I'm disappointed in you."

Julian could not tell from the stern look on Édouard's face whether Berthe's disappointment concerned him or not.

"Is your friend Elizabeth making a mistake, exhibiting at this year's Salon?" Édouard asked.

"That's her decision. But these artists respect you. They are your friends."

"I know, but my work comes first," Édouard said.

"Come, look at my painting," Berthe said, taking Édouard by the hand. "Tell me what you think."

They walked over to the painting where Édouard stood silently gazing at it.

"Tell me what you think," Berthe said.

"I like it very much. But wouldn't you rather have it exhibited at the Salon?"

"If I submitted it, the Salon might reject it. This way people will see and I hope enjoy it."

"That's true, but I think the best way to build your reputation as an artist is to exhibit at the Salon."

Édouard turned from the painting to look out the giant studio window. "It's stopped raining. I think we should go, Julian."

As they walked out of the studio, Julian watched Édouard turn around to look back at Berthe. But she wasn't looking at him.

185

Chapter Forty-Four

A few days later, Édouard and Julian returned to Nadar's studio. They hadn't been there for more than ten minutes when the sound of loud laughter coming from a small group of men and women filled the room. Édouard and Julian slowly walked over to where they thought the laughter was coming from.

Standing in front of Cézanne's "A Modern Olympia," which hung next to Berthe's painting of her sister's newborn, three women in posh hats and decorative dresses were pointing and laughing at Cezanne's tribute to Édouard's painting. Next to them were three well-dressed men who were also laughing.

"A Modern Olympia" was a small painting, less than two feet horizontal and vertical. The painting was of a naked, black woman removing a sheet from a bed, revealing a woman who was also naked. In the foreground, a balding, bearded man sat on a couch watching.

"What was the artist thinking when he painted it?" one woman looking at the painting said.

Édouard and Julian moved closer to the group of men and women standing in front of the painting.

"Do you think he's the painter?" one man said to another. He pointed at the balding man in the foreground of the painting.

All three men were wearing top hats, and frock coats, and carried walking canes. It struck Julian that they were all dressed like Édouard.

Another man pointed to Berthe's painting of her sister

watching over a sleeping child." I don't like this painting either,"
the man said.

"Excuse me, sir," Édouard interrupted. "What don't you like
about that painting?"

"I wasn't talking to you. I'm entitled to my opinion. It's
awful," he said.

"I don't think so," Édouard said.

"Go away and stop annoying me," the man said, speaking
directly at Édouard.

"You should keep your opinion to yourself," Édouard said.
"I don't like it."

"What else don't you like?" the man said.

"If you must know, I don't like the way you dress."

"You don't like the way I'm dressed. Look at you."

"I don't like the way you're dressed," Édouard said again.

"You don't," the man said. He lifted his cane in the air and
brought it down toward Édouard.

Édouard quickly raised his arm to stop the cane. As he did,
Nadar, who had been standing several feet away, marched over,
and stood between them.

"I can handle this, Felix," Édouard said.

"I know you can, Édouard, but this is my studio."

"Your studio?" the man said. "I know you. You're Nadar."

"That's right. Do you want me to take your photograph with
your face all bloody?"

"What are you saying?" the man said.

"That's what will happen if you don't leave right now."

"You can't throw me out."

"I've asked you politely to leave."

"I've paid to be here."

"Are you going to leave, or do I have to throw you out?"

187

"Are you going to leave?" Édouard asked the man.

Nadar quickly grabbed Édouard to hold him back.

"All right. We are. But we have a right to our opinions, and these paintings are the worst."

The man was joined by the rest of the group and walked quietly out of the studio entrance. As they were leaving, Nadar put his arm around Édouard.

"I heard what you said about the way they were dressed," Nadar said. "They dress the same way you do."

"I know that," Édouard said with a smile on his face. "But sometimes, the people who dress the same way as you do are as different as night and day."

"You don't have to tell me," Nadar said.

"Do I need to say more because you may have wondered?" Édouard said. "Fine clothes can make you feel good no matter who you are or what you think."

"I haven't wondered, my friend," Nadar said.

Chapter Forty-Five

Édouard Manet's Journal
June 7, 1874

I painted Berthe again today. She's so spontaneous. I catch her by surprise. She's dressed in black and holding a fan. I capture her loose, black flowing hair. She's wearing a ribbon around her neck. Her pale skin entices me. What am I going to do? I don't know if I'll be able to keep painting her.

We made love in the afternoon in the studio. She tells me she loves me and I tell her I love her. But it's hopeless. We both know we can have nothing real together. I can't give up my family, and that's what I would have to do to make Berthe my own. She says she understands. She wants a family too.

I tell her she should marry my brother Eugene. She's angry at me for saying such a thing. She'd have to get Eugene to ask her. She'd have to flirt with him. Maybe that would work. Would he respond? Could I hide my jealousy? She must think I'm crazy, but I'm not. What am I thinking? What does Eugene think of her? He's never shown an interest. I must convince Berthe that's what she needs to do. Can I bear the pain? Will she know I'll always love her no matter what.

Chapter Forty-Six

In July 1874, Édouard visited Claude Monet, who was living in Argenteuil, a village on the Seine, eight miles from the heart of Paris. The two painters had become close friends, and Édouard had invited Julian to join them that weekend.

Julian took the train from Gare Saint-Lazare to Argenteuil and then walked to Monet's house, just minutes from the train station. When he arrived at the house, Claude and Édouard, who had been waiting outside in the garden, rushed to greet him. Julian stood next to Claude and Édouard looking up at the two-story vine covered building.

"What a beautiful home," he said, looking directly at Claude and wondering if he owned it. Like many other impoverished painters, Julian didn't believe Monet had the money to buy it and knew he often borrowed money from Édouard.

Before Julian could ask if he owned it, Monet spoke up as if he knew what was on Julian's mind. "Édouard helped me get this house," Monet said. "The widow of the former mayor of Argenteuil owns it, and I'm renting it. But someday I'm going to own a house like this."

"The former mayor, "Julian said. "I've always known Édouard has friends in high places."

"I've told you, Julian, my family-owned property in Gennevillers, just across the river. That's how I know the mayor's widow. I'm sure if I had as many friends in high places as you may think I have, all my paintings would win awards at the

Salon."

"None of us have many friends when it comes to the judges at the Salon," Monet said.

"Claude wants to show you around the house," Édouard said.

Julian followed Claude into the house, amazed at how spacious it was. There were several large bedrooms where guests could stay. It had beautiful, polished parquet floors and big windows that let in a lot of light. There was also a garden next to the house from which you could see the river.

When they walked into the living room, Julian saw a ruddy-faced woman he did not know. She looked a little like Édouard's wife, heavy and Dutch. Édouard's brother-in-law, Rudolph Leenhoff, whom Julian knew, was sitting next to the woman.

"Let me introduce you to Marie Macron," Édouard said. "She's from Argenteuil and agreed to pose for me with Rudolph for a painting I'm working on."

She was wearing a flowing striped dress. Julian assumed Édouard had picked it out for her. It didn't seem like a dress she would wear every day. She also had on a blue and white oversized hat. Julian noticed Édouard's brother-in-law was wearing a striped shirt, white trousers, and a straw hat. They also did not seem like something Rudolph would wear either. Julian was sure Édouard had picked those out, too. He often decided on those details for a painting he was working on.

"Let's walk down to the river so I can go back to work," Édouard said. He grabbed his easel standing in the corner of the room and the canvas he was working on. He asked Julian to carry his paint box, brushes, and a pallet.

As they walked toward the river, Julian noticed in the distance several factories, with puffs of smoke rising from them. Much of the area was rural, but Argenteuil was becoming industrialized. What would it be like in ten years? Julian wondered.

When they came to a dock where a boat was tied up, Édouard immediately set the stage for how he wanted the painting to look.

"Would you sit the way you did yesterday?" Édouard said to Rudolph and Marie. He straddled the boat so that he could position them the way he wanted the painting to look. Then he set up his easel and placed the half-finished canvas on it.

Julian walked over to the canvas to look at the painting of Marie and Rudolph together sitting in the boat.

"Look how blue the water is around us," Édouard said.

"It's just how you painted it," Julian said.

They all watched Édouard continue to paint. He was using bright colors laid side by side and kept working for a couple more hours.

"Let's show Julian my boat," Monet said.

"Yes. Let's go to your studio," Édouard said, laughing.

"Okay, my studio," Monet said with a wide grin on his face.

"What do you mean, studio?" Julian asked.

"You'll see," Édouard said.

They walked along the river for about two hundred yards to another dock. There was Monet's boat. He had fitted it out so that he could paint his views of the Seine. There was a little cabin in the stern that protected him from the rain and a tent at the bow that shaded him from the sun.

"Now that you've seen my studio, we can go back to the house and sit down to dinner my wife is preparing."

When they got back to the house, Camille, Monet's wife, was in the kitchen. She had just put a chicken in the oven and was boiling a few potatoes and onions.

"There's nothing better than sitting down to a home cooked

192

meal," Édouard said.

"We're very lucky," Camille said. We have so many vegetables thanks to the Paris sewage pumped across the fields of the next town over."

"Vegetables are grown in a field pumped with sewage. It doesn't matter to me. I'm still hungry." Julian said.

"That's as resourceful as Claude outfitting his boat as his studio. Has Claude taken you out on it?" Julian asked Camille.

"Have we sailed along the Seine in his studio? Yes, we have," Camille said, laughing.

"Of course, we have," Monet said. "It's not just a studio."

"Claude has taken us out twice," Rudolph said.

Édouard had left the living room and then returned carrying with him a painting Julian had never seen before.

"I'm painting more in the open air," Édouard said. "That's something Claude and I have been doing."

He showed Julian a painting of Camille, their son Jean and Monet, in their garden.

"Claude likes it very much," Camille said. "And of course, so do I."

"I've always thought paintings should be what you see and what you feel," Édouard said.

Chapter Forty-Seven

Julian heard the caw, caw, caw of a flock of black crows swooping down from the roof of the building ahead of him. He hated the sound almost as much as much as the rain that had been coming down for days. An occasional rainy day was different; it had the opposite effect. It reinforced Paris's romantic soul because of the colors, and the reflections of light in the streets and in the puddles and the sky, but a constant rain cast a shadow on every one of those days.

Julian headed to Édouard's studio, just three buildings away. It was an unusually cold day in August. The rain had finally stopped that morning, leaving wide puddles of water Julian jumped over trying to avoid. As he got closer to Édouard's building, he saw Berthe leaving. When she reached Julian, he saw she had tears in her eyes.

"Berthe, what's wrong?"

"Nothing, I was supposed to be home hours ago."

"We haven't talked in a while."

"I know. Some other time," she said hurrying down the street.

When Julian reached Édouard's building, he walked up the stairs to his second-floor studio. Édouard was standing in the doorway.

"Did you see Berthe?"

"She seemed in a rush," Julian said as he walked into the studio and sat down on a chair next to the studio's main window.

Julian looked out to the street with a view toward rue Mosnier. It was a new street in the quarter de l'Europe, with no shop fronts, just buildings with many apartments. He looked up at the painting Édouard was working on. It was a portrait of Berthe.

"That's a perfect likeness of Berthe," Julian said.

"I'm in a hurry to get it done. I've been working on it for the last week."

"Why are you in such a hurry?"

"Because once she marries Eugene, I don't think I'll paint another portrait of her."

"You said once she marries your brother? When did she decide on that?"

"Today after she asked me what she should do when Eugene asked her to marry him."

"What did you tell her?"

"I said she should."

"She said that's what she would do and then she ran out of the studio crying."

"Why didn't you run after her?"

"I don't know. I think it's the right decision for her. That's all."

Chapter Forty-Eight

In December 1874, Berthe and Eugene were married. A month after the wedding, Édouard, Suzanne, Julian, and Marlene took the newly married couple to the Palais Garnier to celebrate. By the time they got there, the rain was coming down hard.

"It seems it's always raining ,"Julian said. "Not always, Édouard said "I'll get out first and help the women down."

"My, aren't you the gentleman," Berthe said. She slowly got down from the carriage. Suzanne and Marlene followed. They opened their umbrellas and waited for Eugene and Julian to get down.

"Let's hurry," Eugene said as he took Berthe's hand. "You're getting all wet."

"Aren't you the happy couple?" Julian said to them. Marlene moved close to Julian and he took her arm. Édouard walked over to Suzanne and put his arm around her.

"Yes, let's hurry," Édouard said, barely avoiding a big rain puddle.

Julian and Marlene followed Édouard and Suzanne into the Pavilion des Ambones. It was covered by a giant dome. Julian was mesmerized by a magnificent marble staircase with two flights of stairs leading to the Grand Foyer. They all looked up at the ceiling and then down the hall. It was at least sixty feet from the floor to the ceiling, and the hall had to be more than 500 feet long.

"It is impressive," Eugene said. He smiled at Berthe, who

was still clinging to his arm.

"It's like a palace," she said, her eyes opening wider.

They walked into the horseshoe-shaped theater and found their seats. The canvas stage curtain was painted to look like a draped one with tassels and braid. Above them, a giant bronze and crystal chandelier hung from the ceiling.

"We've got to go backstage to the dance foyer before the program begins," Édouard said. Édouard, Eugene, and Julian got up from their seats and walked to the foyer.

"Marlene, Berthe, and I are going to stay in our seats and read the program," Suzanne said.

When they got to the foyer, Édouard recognized a young woman who was standing alone. "That's Gabrielle Krauss. I saw her perform at the Theatre-Italian in 1867."

"She's beautiful," Julian said.

"Don't stare," Eugene chimed in. "We'll see her perform tonight."

"They say Charles Garnier is going to be here tonight. He's the Opera building architect," Julian said.

"I would think so for the opening night," Édouard said, moving closer to Eugene. Julian heard Édouard whisper to Eugene, "What do you think of married life?"

"Why do you ask? We've only been married a couple of weeks," Eugene said.

"I'd love to know what you would say after ten years. But I'm sure you would still be quite happy then."

"What do you mean?" Julian asked Édouard. He had heard the entire conversation between the two brothers.

"You know what I mean, Julian. Well, maybe you don't. You've never been married."

"Édouard 's a bit of a cynic," Eugene interjected. "But the

women seem to love him."

"That's true but I'm not a cynic."

"Have you ever thought about getting married, Julian?" Eugene asked.

"I have, in fact recently."

"I'm glad to hear that, but we should be getting back to our seats," Édouard said.

Just as soon as they were in their seats, a well-dressed man with a cane walked onto the stage and the audience applauded.

"That's Charles Garnier," Julian said.

"How do you know?" Marlene asked.

"You know because I'm a journalist.

"Is he always that arrogant?" Eugene asked.

"Yes, much of the time, but don't mind," Marlene said.

"Garnier is about to speak. We need to stop talking," Julian said as he reached for Marlene's hand.

"Good evening, ladies and gentlemen. My name is Charles Garnier and I'm very proud of this building." Then he pointed to the chandelier. "That's a work of art but the patrons in the fourth level boxes don't like it because it obstructs their view. We'll have to do something about that."

Garnier continued to provide details about the building. When he was finished, he walked off the stage and the curtain came up. Gabrielle Krauss walked onto the stage and the audience applauded loudly. When she began to sing along with the orchestra, almost everyone in the audience stood up and applauded.

"Isn't her voice just wonderful?" Suzanne said. "I could listen to her all night."

Just minutes after Suzanne spoke, Julian heard a loud cracking sound. He looked up to see Garnier's chandelier begin to pull away from the ceiling.

"We've got to get out of here. It's about to come down on us," Édouard said.

Julian grabbed Marlene. Eugene grabbed Berthe and Édouard pulled Suzanne out of her chair. They all ran into the aisle and out of the theater. Looking back, they saw the chandelier come crashing down. It fell on several people who were sitting close to where they had been sitting.

Julian pulled Édouard aside. "You know there were a few members of the Salon jury in the audience tonight. I think one or two of them had voted to reject your paintings," Julian said, speaking to Édouard as quietly as he could.

"I saw them. What are you getting at?"

"Maybe the chandelier coming down was no accident. I saw someone in the lobby who looked a lot like Pierre, but I wasn't sure it was him and then he disappeared. I wouldn't have said anything if the chandelier hadn't come crashing down."

The three couples left the theater and were trying to get a carriage which proved to be almost impossible. All the theater-goers who had rushed out of the building were also trying to get a carriage. Many of them were talking loudly about the accident and their escape. Julian heard one man name two of the people who had been struck by the crashing chandelier. But he did not think they were the names of any Salon jury members. An hour later, Julian was able to hail down a carriage.

The next day, Édouard and Julian were at the café Guerbois to have lunch. Gustav, who often waited on them, came to their table with a newspaper in his hand.

"Good morning, Gustav," Édouard. "What do you have there?"

Gustav pointed to an article in the newspaper and Édouard

began to read it. The article was about a man who was killed the week before when the carriage he was driving and had stolen, overturned and killed him. The man was trying to escape from the police who wanted to arrest him for attempting to murder a man who was a member of the Salon jury. The police identified the man who was killed when the carriage overturned. His name was Pierre Pelleton.

"Wasn't he the man who often came here with you, Édouard?" Gustav asked.

"That's terrible," Édouard said. "And yes, he was."

"I thought so."

"I had known him for years. He was the subject of one of my paintings."

"The last time we saw him, he told us he had a wife and a child," Julian said.

"He cared very much about his family. Maybe he was trying to take care of his wife and child," Édouard said.

Chapter Forty-Nine

Two years after Berthe and Eugene were married, Marlene and Julian visited the 1876 Salon which had rejected two of Édouard's paintings.

As they strolled through the galleries, studying each painting, Julian wondered why they were considered better than the two paintings Édouard submitted.

Julian and Marlene continued to stroll through the galleries, finally coming to the last room. As Julian entered the room, he was surprised to see Victorine standing in front of her portrait.

"Victorine, is that you?" Julian said, looking pleased to see her.

"Yes. In the flesh and that is my portrait," she said.

"That portrait of you is very good and I assume you painted it."

"Yes, it is very good," Marlene said.

"Yes, I painted it and I kept my clothes on," Victorine said.

"Let me introduce you to Marlene. She also likes your portrait."

"Very pleased to meet you."

"It's a pleasure to meet you," Marlene said.

"Édouard's not with you?" Victorine asked.

"No. He's miserable about the Salon rejecting his paintings this year. Did you find someone who could teach you more about painting?" Julian asked.

"Édouard didn't want to, so yes, I did. His name is Etienne

Leroy."

"I've not heard of him."

"You haven't? He's exhibited at the Salon each year for the last fifteen."

"From your self-portrait, I would say he's an excellent teacher."

"Yes, he is. I've learned a lot from him in a very short time."

"The catalog has over 4,000 paintings," Julian said.

"That's right. I'm surprised the Salon rejected Édouard paintings again."

"You know as well as anyone that there are many people that don't like Édouard's paintings."

"Yes. And I know how cruel they can be."

"Yes, you do."

Victorine gazed at Marlene and Julian. "You look very nice together," Victorine said. "Are you married?"

"No, we're not," Marlene said.

"It was rude of me to ask."

"No, it wasn't," Julian said.

"Tell me about Édouard. I sometimes miss modeling for him."

"You do?"

"Yes. Sometimes it was nice."

"Did you know one of Édouard 's models married his brother, Eugene?"

"Yes. I heard. Berthe Morisot. I understand, she's also a painter."

"Yes, and like you, a very good one."

"What does Édouard think about his brother marrying her? I've heard some awful gossip about it."

"You have?"

"I've heard some people say that she couldn't have Édouard, so, she married his brother instead."

"Yes. I've heard that too, but it's certainly not true." Marlene said.

"Édouard told me he suggested it to Eugene," Julian said.

"He did?"

"That's what he told me."

"That's strange. So how is Édouard doing?"

"You may have read about it. He put together an exhibit of his paintings at his studio. I think today was the last day."

"Yes, I read about that.".

"He sent invitations that said he wanted people to do him the honor of coming to see the paintings rejected by the 1876 jury."

"How was the turnout?"

"Hundreds, every day."

"That's good."

"As you know, it can sometimes be bad," Julian said. "The more people who go to the exhibition, the more critics come. One critic wrote that since Édouard wants our opinion, we want to tell him he has the eye of a painter but none of his soul."

"These critics are just cruel," Marlene said.

"They can be if they don't understand," Victorine said.

"I sometimes think they don't want to understand," Julian said.

"What do you do?" Victorine asked Marlene.

"I'm a portrait photographer. Perhaps I could photograph you."?

"I'd like that."

As they talked, several people walked over to Victorine's painting.

"Is that you?" one man asked Victorine.

203

"Yes. What do you think?"

"It's an excellent likeness," the man said.

Julian was surprised not one of the people who viewed the painting seemed to recognize Victorine as Édouard's model for Olympia. Otherwise, he thought they would have treated her as they had in the past, as a prostitute. But now she was being recognized as a painter.

Chapter Fifty

When Marlene and Julian got back to the apartment from the Salon, Julian went to the study and sat down at his desk to continue working on his novel. He had put it aside several years before, frustrated, but Marlene had convinced him to finish it. She came into the studio and sat down in the chair next to Julian's desk.

"I'm glad you went back to working on it again," she said. "You are going to finish it."

"I know. It's about time I finished something," Julian said.

She picked up the last couple of pages he had been working on and read them.

"Julian. It's very good. It's better than Flaubert."

"I owe it all to your, Marlene."

"No you don't. You owe it to yourself."

Julian was just getting up from his desk when he heard someone at the front door. Julian opened it and Édouard was standing there. His studio was just a few doors down from Julian's apartment on rue Saint-Pétersbourg.

"Did you go to the Salon today?" Édouard asked.

"Édouard, come in. Yes. Why?"

"I heard Victorine had a painting in the exhibit."

"Yes. Marlene and I saw her there."

Marlene walked over to where Édouard and Julian were standing. "Won't you sit down, Édouard?" she said.

"It's too late now, but I think you should have helped

Victorine become a painter," Julian said.

"Maybe you're right. Maybe I should have."

"She asked about you," Julian said.

"What did you tell her?"

"I told her about Eugene and Berthe getting married. She had heard about it."

"What did she think?"

"She seemed surprised when I told her you suggested to Eugene that he marry Berthe."

"She did?"

"Yes, she did."

"Did you talk about anything else?"

"We talked about your exhibit."

"You did?"

"I told her about the critic who wrote that you have the eye of a painter but none of his soul."

"I don't think that critic has a soul."

"You know what surprised me?" Julian said.

"What?"

"The people we saw viewing Victorine's painting didn't seem to recognize her."

"That's a good thing," Édouard said. "She's been treated very badly , I know. People have been very unfair to her. But what else did she have to say?"

"She was interested in whether Marlene and I were married."

"I've often wondered when you two were going to get married."

"I don't enjoy talking about marriage. It's something I haven't come to grips with yet," Julian said.

"Would you like me to change the subject? All right, I'll change the subject. How's your novel coming along?" Édouard asked.

"Marlene pushed me to finish it, which got me to wondering. How are you able to finish every painting you start?"

"I don't finish everyone I start, but I do get wrapped up in them, and so most of the time I feel compelled to finish."

"It's a good feeling every time you finish one?"

"Yes. It's my reason for living. Painting is my life."

It was nearly midnight when Édouard said it was time for him to go home. After Édouard left, Marlene walked over to Julian, gave him a long kiss on the lips, and then looked into his eyes. "You really have to be just as ambitious as Édouard," she said.

"I know I need to be and with you around, I will be."

Chapter Fifty-One

Édouard, was forty-six when he painted his self-portrait. It was also about that time he complained about what he thought might be rheumatism.

Julian met Édouard one morning at his studio. Édouard was at work on his self-portrait. Julian watched Édouard looking at himself in a full-size mirror standing next to his easel.

"I've finished my novel and now I have find a publisher," Julian said.

"I'm sure it won't be difficult for you to find one."

Julian looked at the painting. "It's an excellent likeness."

"I wish I could sit when I paint, but I can't. It's getting more difficult to stand."

"Why's that?"

"I don't know. I have a great deal of pain in my legs," Édouard said. "What did Dr. Sireday have to say about it?" Julian asked.

"He recommended hydrotherapy. But I'd have to go to Bellevue and stay there for a few weeks."

"If that's what the doctor thinks will help, go to Bellevue."

"I know."

Julian looked again at the portrait. It certainly was Édouard. It was Édouard as a painter, dressed for the boulevard, wearing a bowler and his camel-colored coat.

"It reminds me of the painting by Diego Velazquez we viewed at the Prado in Madrid. I think it was called The Ladies in Waiting.

"Yes. But Velázquez's painting was more than a self-portrait. There was a royal family standing around him."

"You don't have a royal family standing around you."

"True."

"Do you remember what year we went to Madrid?"

"It was 1865, the year we met Theodore Duret at that restaurant."

"Yes. I remember. You kept ordering different dishes."

"Each time I rejected a dish as inedible, I sent the waiter away for another one. The food was dreadful. Duret would call the waiter back each time. He enjoyed every one of those dishes."

"You thought he was making fun of you?"

"Yes. But he wasn't."

"Before the day was over, we were all friends."

"I painted his portrait a few years later."

"He's a talented journalist. Maybe he'll write your biography."

"Maybe."

Édouard quickly changed the subject. "How are you and Marlene doing?"

"Fine. Why do you ask?"

"I just wondered. That's all."

"Have you heard from Eugene and Berthe?"

"Yes. They sent me a photograph of their daughter, Julie."

Édouard went to a desk in a corner of the studio and brought back a framed photograph of Julie. Julian looked at the desk and realized there were no other photographs.

"She looks just like her mother," Édouard said.

Julian looked at the photograph and was surprised at the girl's strong resemblance to Édouard. "Yes, she looks just like

Berthe," Julian said.

Édouard went back to working on his self-portrait. But minutes later, he dropped his brush and let out a scream.

"I can't take it anymore."

"What's wrong?" Julian asked.

"It's my legs," he said. "The pain is awful."

"You must go to Bellevue for the therapy.

"I will. I don't want to end up like my father."

Julian heard a knock on the studio door and went to see who it was. Suzanne was standing there.

"Good morning, Julian. I came to see how Édouard's portrait is coming along."

"Do you like it, Suzanne?" Édouard asked.

She was silent for a moment. "Very much, but why did you decide to paint it now? I've asked you many times when were you going to paint a self-portrait and you've said it wasn't the right time, "Suzanne said.

"Now is just as good a time as any."

"How are your legs?" Suzanne asked. There was a worried look on her face.

"They're bothering me some. I need to do something about it."

"Dr. Sireday said you need to go to Bellevue," she said.

"I know. I will."

Chapter Fifty-Two

Although Édouard agreed to go to Bellevue for therapy, he waited. Julian visited him a few weeks after he had moved into a new studio on Rue d' Amsterdam. The walls were covered with paintings that seemed to sum up Édouard's life. Framed and unframed paintings hung next to each other. It was like a Salon exhibition. There were even more paintings stacked against the walls and others were on easels.

This new studio was where Édouard's circle of friends, other painters, writers, and collectors whom he used to meet at the Café Nouvelle-Athens, would now gather. Édouard found it harder and harder to walk to the café because of his aliment. So, his friends started meeting at the studio.

Julian arrived around six o'clock that evening. They sat in chairs at a large table that could accommodate a dozen people in a corner of the studio. Édouard was surrounded by five of his friends, including Julian. Theodore Duret puffed on a cigar. Édouard Duranty, the critic Édouard dueled with, now a close friend leaned back in his chair. Henri-Fantin-Latour, the painter who introduced Édouard and Julian to Berthe Morisot, sat with one elbow on the table and sipped a glass of wine. Nadar was the fifth person. He nursed a glass of beer and would stand up and then sit down several times in an hour.

"How can someone who has not lived it write an honest account of history?" Nadar asked.

Duranty jumped into the conversation. "What are you talking

about?"

"There's an Englishman who's written an account of the Siege of Paris and the Commune. He never lived through it. How can it be accurate?" Nadar asked.

Duranty jumped in again. "There are journals he's probably read. He's likely interviewed people from both sides, French and Prussian. That's the way history is written, whether it happened ten or two hundred years ago."

"But it's still through the Englishman's eyes," Nadar insisted. "He determines what's relevant and what's not. That's my point."

"What if you were to write it? You would tell it through the eyes of a French man. Would it be any more accurate?" Nadar defended his position. "Not necessarily. The Englishman may have a point of view that could cloud an accurate account."

"So, history is one man's point of view?" Fantin-Latour asked.

"That's the way I see it," Nadar said. "It's like a photograph. What you see is one man's point of view. That's how he sees the subject."

"That's the problem with the art critics writing for these journals," Édouard interjected. "They're looking at my work through their eyes and from a historical perspective. They're not looking through the artist's eyes."

"It's the same with the Salon jury," Fantin-Latour added.

"That's right," Édouard said.

"Speaking about the jury, I'd like to know, Édouard, if you have heard about your proposal for decorating the Hotel de Ville council chamber?" Duret said.

"No, and I'm angry about that."

"What did you propose?" Fantin-Latour asked.

"I sent a letter to the prefect suggesting I do a series of compositions. They would represent the various aspects of life in Paris."

"What do you mean?" Fantin-Latour asked.

"The Paris markets, railway, port, race courses, and gardens. I also wanted to create a gallery focused on the men who are contributing to the importance and prosperity of Paris."

"What happened to your proposal?"

"It was treated like one of my paintings rejected by the Salon jury. Only I didn't even get the courtesy of a negative reply."

The conversation continued for another hour. By then, Édouard looked exhausted. He had closed his eyes several times.

"Anything wrong?" Julian asked Édouard.

"My legs are bothering me," Édouard said. "As always, this has been stimulating, but would you gentlemen be so kind as to let me retire?"

Within minutes, everyone had left the studio, except for Julian. "Are you all right?" Julian asked Édouard.

"It's my left foot. It aches," Édouard said. "I don't know if it's rheumatism or something else."

"Édouard. You need to get to go for treatment," Julian said.

"I know and I'll go."

Chapter Fifty-Three

In September 1879, Édouard went to Bellevue for treatment. He took therapeutic showers and messages four to five hours a day. He hoped the therapy would help improve his balance and coordination and lessen the pain in his legs, but the treatment was torture.

Édouard rented a villa where his friends and family could visit during the treatment. One day, Julian visited him. That same day, Leon and Lily came to see him. They sat in the main room of the villa. Édouard had just spent five hours in therapy.

"Lily's expecting," Leon said. "I guess you can see that."

It was the first time Édouard had heard about the baby. He looked at Leon with a wide smile on his face. "That's wonderful news," Édouard said."

Lily was almost giggling. "If it's a boy, we'd like to name the baby after you, Monsieur Manet."

"You would? Surely there's someone in your family, Lily, for you to name the baby after."

"No," Leon interrupted. "Lily and I have talked it over, and we'd like to name the baby after you."

Suzanne, who had been in the kitchen, came into the room. "This is an unexpected pleasure. I didn't know you were going to be here", she said.

"We wanted to surprise you both," Leon said.

"Did I hear you say you want to name your baby after Édouard?" Suzanne asked.

"That's right," Lily said. "And if it's a girl, we want to name her Suzanne after you." "Yes," Leon said. "We've talked that over, too."

"That's very nice for you to want to do that," Suzanne said. She looked directly at Édouard. "What do you think?"

"It's fine if that's what Leon and Lily want."

"That's great. That's what Lily and I want."

"I think this calls for a celebration," Édouard said.

"I'll get a bottle of wine," Suzanne said. She came back with an open bottle and four empty glasses on a tray. Édouard filled the glasses and handed one to Leon, Lily, and Suzanne.

"Here's to the baby and to mother and father," Édouard said as he raised his glass.

"Yes. Here's to our family," Leon said.

Just as the room had gotten quiet, there was a knock on the door. It was Nadar. He hurried in and smiled at Lily.

"It looks like you're expecting," Nadar said with a smile on his face.

"I am," Lily said.

Nadar walked over to Leon and shook his hand. "Congratulations."

"Thank you," Leon said.

"We were just talking about what name to give the baby," Lily said.

Édouard shuddered. He wiped his brow with a handkerchief he pulled from his trouser pocket.

"How are you feeling, Édouard?" Nadar asked.

"I'm doing fine. I think the therapy is helping, and this good news makes me feel better."

Chapter Fifty-Four

Édouard Manet's Journal
December 28, 1880

It's been five years since Berthe married my brother. I stopped her a few streets away from their home. I asked her to come to my studio alone. I had a gift I wanted to give her for New Year's. She was excited and agreed to meet me there.

I've seen her many times since she married, but never alone. I wouldn't want Eugene to know, although maybe he might not think anything of it.

I still have such strong feelings for her. I've never stopped loving her. I've tried to stop. Why can't I stop thinking about her? I could understand it if she were my first love. They say you never forget your first love, but she wasn't. I can't remember my first love.

I kissed her. She hesitated for a moment and then kissed me back. We walked over to the easel I had bought her as a gift.

"This is for you. I can't give you a necklace of pearls or a locket, although I wish I could."

"It came from you. It means everything."

"What are we going to do?"

She was quiet for a moment and then told me this would be the last time we could see each other alone. It was like the thunder you hear during a storm. You hear it many times, not just once. "Even though I want you, I can't have you." She said it once, but

I heard it many times.

I pressed her against me, thinking it would be the last time I could show her how much she meant to me. How warm we felt together in each other's arms. But I knew it was over. I would never paint her or make love to her again.

Chapter Fifty-Five

In May 1881, when Édouard was fifty years old, he was awarded a second-class medal for his portrait of de M. Prettiest, the lion hunter, at the Salon that year. When an artist was awarded the medal, the government conferred on him the Legion of Honor. If an artist was awarded the Legion of Honor, he could exhibit his paintings at every subsequent Salon. No painting could be rejected.

Édouard and Julian arrived at the Salon just before the jury was to take its first vote. The jury passed through the gallery and then gathered in front of the painting as part of the process to come up with a preliminary list of nominees. To be included on the preliminary list, one-third of the twenty-four members of the jury had to approve of the painting. The artists to be awarded the medal were chosen by a second and majority vote.

It was an exhausting procedure, Julian thought as he and Édouard watched the jury file past the portrait and then gather several feet away to discuss and vote on the painting. After about half an hour, one of the jury members came back to speak with Édouard.

"You've made the first list," the man said. "We'll be back to view the portrait again for a final vote."

Édouard let out a sigh of relief. He had gained the respect of some members of the jury, but knew there were others who saw him as someone trying to crush century-old traditions.

"My art is different. When I see a woman, I conjure up an

image."

"It's the same for me, When I watch something happening, I see a story for a novel. But it's not what happened. It's beyond that."

"I want to be recognized; I can't deny that," Édouard said. "But just to have the public view my work, to understand and appreciate it, gives me the greatest satisfaction."

Édouard and Julian stood waiting for the members of the jury to come back. About half an hour later, the jury returned. This time, Julian and Édouard could hear a few loud voices. It seemed like some of the jury members were arguing with each other. A few minutes later, one member of the jury walked back to speak with Édouard.

"There was some strong opposition," he said. "You were two votes short."

"I didn't get a majority?"

"No. You did after one member of the jury convinced two others. Congratulations."

"Can you tell me the names of the jury members who voted yes?"

The man handed Édouard a paper with the names of the jury members who voted for him. Édouard looked down at the paper and then walked toward the group and thanked each jury member who voted for him.

"You've conquered the Salon," Julian said, looking directly at Édouard.

Chapter Fifty-Six

In November, the government conferred on Édouard the Legion of Honor. No longer could the Salon reject his paintings. The next month, Édouard began work on a new painting, "A Bar at the Folies-Bergère." Édouard asked Lily to pose as a barmaid for the painting.

Leon and Lily arrived with their new baby at Édouard's studio early that morning. Julian was already there, setting up some props for the painting.

"I'm so pleased you named your baby after me," Édouard said.

"We are too," Lily said, placing the baby in a crib Édouard brought to the studio.

Édouard set up his easel and sat down to paint. He could no longer stand to paint because of the pain in his legs.

"What do you think?" Édouard asked Leon.

"It's as if we were at the Folies-Bergère."

"Yes."

Édouard walked over to Lily and lifted her chin up.

"I want you to look directly at me," Édouard said. "I want you to look at me with your eyes wide open."

After three hours, Lily's eyes began to tear. She blinked several times, again and again.

"I'm almost through with you for the day. I'm going to work on the background."

Édouard began to paint a well-dressed man wearing a top hat

in one corner of the painting. The man was reflected in a mirror, looking directly at a second image of Lily. It was the reflection of her back. She was gazing at the man.

"That's an interesting perspective," Julian said.

"Yes. It's my perspective," Édouard said.

Chapter Fifty-Seven

Between 1859 and 1882, eight annual Salons rejected Édouard's paintings, and thirteen exhibited them. His painting of the "Bar at the Folies-Bergère" was being exhibited at the 1882 Salon.

The day it opened, Édouard, Marlene, and Julian got there early. Julian had told Marlene about the painting, but she had not seen it yet.

The rain was coming down quite hard on their way to the studio. Marlene jumped out of the carriage while Julian waited for Édouard, who limped along with his cane.

"I hate this blasted rain," Édouard muttered. "It chills me to the bone."

Julian, with his right hand on Édouard's shoulder, helped him walk to the gallery, where his paintings hung. Édouard was now among the select. His paintings with the inscription on the frame designating the artist's unique status were on exhibit for everyone to see, the critics who questioned his work as an artist and the people who laughed at his paintings. It was recognition no one could take away.

A group of people who had come into the gallery looked up at Édouard's paintings. One man in the group pointed to the inscription on the frame. Julian saw how the inscription shaped their reaction to Édouard and his work. Unlike in the past, they were not laughing. As they glared at "Bar at the Folies-Bergère," Julian heard a woman speak to the man who had pointed to the inscription.

"What does this painting mean?" she said.

"I don't know, but it is the work of an artist. I know that," the man said with no hesitation.

"It's hard to tell. But it is very good, and I admire the artist who painted it," the woman said.

Édouard, who had also heard the conversation, looked at Julian and whispered, "See? They're not laughing anymore."

"No, they're not," Julian said.

The group moved over to the other painting, "Jeanne." It was a half-length portrait of a girl in a flowered dress, with a hat, holding an umbrella in her hand. It had the same inscription on the frame as Édouard's other painting.

"This one is wonderful," the woman said.

"Yes, it is," another man in the group said.

After spending a few hours at the Salon and watching many of the people admire Édouard's paintings, they left and hailed a carriage. As he was climbing into the carriage, Édouard trembled.

"I think I'm going to pass out," he said.

Marlene helped Julian get Édouard into the carriage, laying him down on the seat. He was talking but making no sense. His head dropped forward, his muscles tensed up, and it looked like Édouard was having a seizure.

"Édouard. What's wrong?" Marlene said as a tear rolled down her cheek.

Édouard had passed out, and Marlene lifted his head onto her lap. She was crying. It was her sensitive side Julian had rarely seen. He had asked her why. She told him she often felt vulnerable when she showed emotion. But she promised Julian she would try to be more open. After that promise, he knew they had a future together.

"We need to get him to a doctor," Julian shouted to the

driver.

"What's wrong with him?" the driver asked.

"We don't know," Marlene said. "Please hurry." The driver pushed the horses harder. When they got to Dr. Sireday's office, Édouard 's eyes were open. He was flushed and sweating but he managed to sit up and speak coherently.

"What happened?" he asked.

"We think you had a seizure," Julian said. "We're at Dr. Sireday's office."

Julian told Édouard to put one arm around his shoulder and the other around Marlene's, and they walked him to the office. Dr. Sireday opened the door and helped them get Édouard seated in a chair.

"Did he have a seizure?" Dr. Sireday asked.

"We think so," Julian said.

"It's the ergot," Dr. Sireday said. "I told him to stop taking it."

"What do you mean? "Julian asked.

"Some doctor told him it would help with his walking, but it didn't."

"Why does he keep taking it? "

"I don't know. I told him it was very bad. It constricts the blood vessels and can lead to gangrene."

Édouard looked up from the chair. He had a questioning look on his face.

"I thought it would help," he said.

"But the doctor said it won't," Marlene said.

"You've got to stop taking it," Julian said.

"He'll be all right for now. You can take him home," Dr. Sireday said.

Marlene and Julian helped Édouard up and walked him to

the street. It took them ten minutes before they could hail a carriage. When they got him home, Suzanne helped get Édouard to his bed.

"Is he going to be all right?" she asked.

"Yes," Julian said. "But make sure he doesn't take any more of that ergot."

"He's stubborn, but I will make sure he doesn't," Suzanne said.

Chapter Fifty-Eight

In August 1882, Julian met Édouard at the home of Eugene Labiche in Rueil, just outside Paris. Édouard had gone there with his family, hoping he would feel better being in such a tranquil place.

Labiche was a comic playwright Édouard had known for years. It never ceased to amaze Julian at the number of friends Édouard had. There were so many well-known poets and painters, novelists and composers, sculptors and actors.

Julian met Édouard in the garden in front of the house, sitting on a bench in the shade. His easel with a canvas was in front of him. He was working on a painting of Labiche's home, a two-story cottage that captured Julian's attention.

"I get a warm feeling just being here," Julian said.

"Yes, I feel good being here. I love the house and I enjoy being in the open air."

"Are Suzanne and Leon and Lily here?"

"They went to the city today, but they're returning tomorrow."

Édouard put down his brush and the palette he was holding and bent over to rub his legs.

"They're still giving you trouble?"

"Yes, but I've gotten off the ergot. It wasn't helping me at all."

"I told you to stop taking it."

"It was probably the worst thing I could do to myself."

"Is Monsieur Labiche here? It would be a real privilege to meet him."

"No, he's in Sologne. He has another home there."

"Do you know him well?"

"Yes. As you know, he's well known for his comedies. I don't know if many people know he studied law."

"I didn't know that. I've seen his plays. They're quite good."

"Yes, he's a very good playwright."

"Why would such a great writer want to study law?"

"It's complicated. He had his first short story published when he was just twenty and wrote a very good romance novel, but his publisher went bankrupt."

"So, what did he want to do after that?"

"That's when he started writing comedies. But the parents of the woman he wanted to marry didn't think much of comedy writers. He had to promise he would renounce writing comedies and pursue a law career."

"That's a little like what happened with you and your father."

"I guess you could say that. As you know very well, my father finally let me pursue my desire to become a painter. All I had to do was fail the naval exam a second time, just as you did."

"What happened with Monsieur Labiche?"

"After a year, his wife stepped in and released him from his promise. I wish my mother had done that for me."

"I never knew you felt that way."

"That was a long time ago. But I didn't ask you to come to talk about Monsieur Labiche."

"I know. You wanted to talk with me about your will."

"Yes. I'm going to make Suzanne the primary beneficiary. When she dies, she'll leave whatever's left to Leon."

"And what about your paintings?"

"The pictures, sketches, and drawings in my studio are to be sold at auction I want Theodore Duret to take charge of the sale. You don't mind, do you, Julian? I want you to choose whatever painting you want."

"No. I understand."

"He's been a good friend, and I trust his taste. He'll know what should be put up for auction and what should be destroyed."

"What about the proceeds?"

"Fifty thousand francs are to go to Leon. The rest to Suzanne. When I go back to Paris, I want you to witness my will. Will you do that?"

"Of course."

"Will you carry the easel to the house? I'll take the canvas."

"Of course."

When they got to the house, they went into the main room.

"Can you go into the kitchen? There are a couple of bottles of wine. And there are some wine glasses in the cabinet near the sink. Can you bring those too? My leg continues to bother me."

Julian went into the kitchen, found a corkscrew in one of the cabinet drawers, and opened a bottle of wine. He found a tray and took down a couple of glasses from the cabinet.

"Just like old times," Julian said as he walked back into the main room.

"Yes. Just like old times."

Julian heard a carriage stop outside in front of the house and heard a woman's voice. She was thanking the driver. He looked to see who it was. It was Berthe.

"Maybe you can get that carriage to take you back to Paris," Édouard said to Julian as Berthe walked into the room.

"Yes. I'll run and get it. Hello, Berthe."

"Hello, Julian."

"I'll see you back in Paris, Julian," Édouard said.

228

Chapter Fifty-Nine

Édouard returned to Paris on September 27 and went to his lawyer's office to draft his will. Julian went with him to witness the document. In the carriage on their way to the office, Julian asked him about his visit with Berthe.

"It was very nice. She came alone because Eugene was away on business, and she was concerned about me."

Julian nodded and didn't ask anything more about Berthe's visit. Over the years, he had become used to Édouard's discretion about his relationship with Berthe.

They walked into the lawyer's office, and Édouard sat down to write out his will. It was exactly as he had told Julian. He was leaving everything to Suzanne, who would bequeath what was left to Leon when she died. Julian witnessed the will, and then they left the lawyer's office and returned to Édouard's studio.

The two friends sat in Édouard's studio looking out the giant windows, watching the rain come down.

"Do you remember the day we met?" Édouard asked.

"Yes. It was pouring rain."

"Do you remember the time we spent in Rio?"

"Yes. It was hard for you to keep track of the time, especially when you were with that young woman, Clarissa. Wasn't that her name? Your sketch of Clarissa really captured her."

"Yes. That was her name. It was such a beautiful name and she was too. I still have the sketch. Maybe I should use it as the subject of a painting to exhibit at the 1883 Salon. I have nothing else to send."

"I'm sure you'll come up with something."

"Yes. I'll try now that my paintings can never be rejected by the Salon."

"What about the 1884 Salon?"

"I have some ideas."

Julian left the studio and told Édouard he would be back every day. But each day Julian visited him, it was clear Édouard didn't have the energy to begin another great painting. Instead, he began spending hours reading. In a small way, it was a distraction from the pain he was suffering.

One day, Julian went to Édouard's studio, and the painter told him he had a letter for him to read after his death.

"That could be years," Julian said.

"No. It could be months."

"What's in the letter?"

"You'll find out."

Julian looked at Édouard for at least a minute. Édouard sat back in his chair and smiled.

"Why not tell me about it now?" Julian asked.

"Because when it's time, that's when I want to be sure you'll read it."

"I will."

"It's something I must share with you."

"We've been friends for so many years."

"Yes."

"But friends don't keep secrets."

"Yes, they do."

Julian gave up trying to find out what was in the letter. "I'll find out when it's time," he said.

Chapter Sixty

Édouard's illness continued to affect his ability to walk. He could no longer go to his studio, even with a cane, and now he spent much of his time at his apartment. He was in constant pain. He continued to believe the ergot would help and he lied that he had stopped taking it

For the next twelve days, Édouard stayed at his apartment. The day Julian visited him, his leg had turned black, gangrene. He'd been in bed for eight days.

"Have you come to say goodbye?" Édouard said.

"Why do you say that?"

"You haven't seen my leg."

"No. I haven't."

"They may have to cut it off."

Édouard reached across the bed to the nightstand next to it and pulled open the drawer. He lifted a large envelope from the drawer and handed it to Julian.

"Here's the letter I promised. I hope it will mean something to you when you read it."

"Of course, it will."

Julian reached over to touch Édouard's cheek and slowly walked out of the room with the envelope under his arm.

On April 20, Édouard's leg had to be amputated. Gangrene had set in For the next ten days, Édouard ran a fever and then went into a coma. Many of his friends came to see him, but he didn't know they were there. He died on the evening of April 30.

Although Édouard declined the offer of the Archbishop of Paris administering extreme unction, Leon asked, and it was given in Édouard's last hours.

Édouard was buried on May 3. At noon, the bells of the church of Saint-Louis d'Antin tolled as the procession emerged from the church. The pallbearers were followed by Suzanne and Leon and Lily, Édouard's mother, and Berthe and Eugene Manet. The streets were lined with people as the carriage carrying Édouard's casket made its way to Passy cemetery.

At the gravesite, Theodore Duret, was the first to speak.

"Édouard saw the world in a brilliance of light to which other eyes were blind. He transferred on canvas the sensations which were flashed upon his eye."

"Édouard was a Parisian of Parisians, both in his habits and in his attitude towards life. He possessed the mundane temperament, the artistic sensibility, the delight of social intercourse – all of those qualities which give the Parisian his distinguishing air of refinement."

Antonin Proust, who had been Minister of Arts and was instrumental in Édouard being awarded the Legion of Honor spoke after Duret.

"It is with deep feelings that I speak over the grave that carries away a master of French art and, in the same moment, separates us from a devoted friend."

"The injustice of critics destroyed Édouard's life, despite his great courage. Along with unfinished lifework, he leaves a wife and a son, who during the long hours of his agony showed their admirable devotion."

Standing close to each other at the gravesite, Marlene whispered to Julian. "Aren't you going to speak?"

"No. Everything has been said," Julian said, as they walked

arm in arm up to the casket and placed a rose on it before it was lowered into the ground.

"It's hard for me to get used to the idea that I won't see him anymore," Julian said.

"I know, but you'll see him in his paintings."

Julian reached into his coat pocket and pulled out the envelope with the letter Édouard gave him.

"What's that?" Marlene asked.

"It's Édouard's letter to me."

Julian opened the envelope, unfolded the letter, and read it.

September 28, 1882

My Dear Julian,

I have told you many times that it's not the number of years you're on this earth that matters, but what you do with the time you're here. I hope you will always remember that because it will help ensure that you will be the great novelist you have always wanted to be.

But there's something else that's just as important and it's not even the love of a woman. There were many for me, but I really only loved one woman.

Suzanne was my wife and was so important in my life. But there was someone else I loved more. You always knew who she was, but you never spoke about it to anyone and for that I'm grateful.

I hope that by now you also know what is as important as what you do with your life; it is family. Because of family, I could have never left Suzanne or Leon. I know you may think it's strange for me to say, but it is true. I hope that one day you will have a family.

We've had a great friendship and because of that, you know more about me than anyone else. Maybe someday you'll write about that friendship. So, I'm leaving my journals with you, and you can do what

233

you wish with them. I don't think most people truly understood me and my work. Maybe you can explain it better than I ever could. Goodbye, my dear friend. I hope life continues to be good to you.

Édouard

When Julian finished reading the letter, he looked at Marlene.

"What did *Édouard* want you to know?" Marlene asked.

"That there was nothing more important to him than family; I think he was telling me it should be just as important to me."

"I 've always known that about you. And Édouard did too. I think he wanted to remind you."

Epilogue

A few years later, Marlene and Julian, who had published three novels by then, were married. They had just a few friends at the wedding. Nadar was there, as well as Berthe and Eugene, Suzanne, Leon and Lily.

Nadar was writing again. A year after Édouard died, he wrote about Leon Gambetta, who left Paris in a balloon during the Franco Prussian-War, and when he got to Tours, took control as Minister of the Interior and of War; it was a highly blasphemous skit. Nadar also finished writing a study of his old socialist friend Louis Blanc who had favored reforms to guarantee employment for the poor.

Julian attended the 1885 Salon and saw Victorine. She was exhibiting one of her paintings. She told Julian a few months after Édouard died, she had written to Suzanne seeking some help because she had fallen on hard times. Years before, when she returned to Paris from America, Édouard promised to reward her. But she turned him down then. Instead, she told him that when she could no longer pose, she would take him up on his offer. Suzanne never answered Victorine's letter.

Leon and Lily had another child, a daughter. They named her Suzanne. Julian and Marlene went to see them a couple of times when Suzanne was there. Suzanne doted over her granddaughter. Leon took up painting. Some of his paintings were so good Julian thought Édouard could have painted them.

During the winter of 1883-84, Berthe, who continued to

paint, organized an exhibition and later the sale of some of Édouard's works at the Palais des Beaux-Arts. She along with, Claude Monet and John Singer Sargent, raised 20,000 francs and bought "Olympia" from Suzanne. It was hung in the Musee de Luxembourg.

Printed in the USA
CPSIA information can be obtained
at www.ICGtesting.com
LVHW091117270324
775617LV00001B/5